RELUCTANT
CHRISTMAS

A Willow Bay Novel

by Laurie Ryan

www.laurieryanauthor.com

Copyright

Reluctant Christmas, Book 5 of the Willow Bay series, Copyright © 2022 Laurie Ryan All rights reserved
ebook ISBN: 979-8-9859122-1-0
Print ISBN: 979-8-9859122-2-7
Editor: Libby Doyle, Fairhill Editing
Cover design: C. Friesen at DefianceBooks.com

Learn more about Laurie Ryan and her books at **www.laurieryanauthor.com** and for up-to-date information about releases, please consider joining Laurie's **mailing list** through her website.

Dedication

To my mother, who always made Christmas the most special day of the year. Happy Christmas in heaven, Mom!

Chapter One

Dr. Grace Benson was done with people not listening to her. Just five hours into her twelve-hour night shift in the ER, and she'd already had to deal with an old man with dementia and no pants who wandered out before she could treat him for a raging UTI—she'd put the cops onto that search—and a drunk teenager who'd felt her up while she was sticking a gastric tube down his throat to pump his stomach. She couldn't do her job if people didn't do what they were told.

Grace passed a tree in the lobby, emblazoned with lights and holiday decorations. Christmas. One more thing to endure.

The nurse's station was, thankfully, mostly vacant, except for the garland everywhere. Grace sank into a chair, relieved to be off her feet for a few minutes. She slipped out of her crocs and almost groaned in pleasure, not sure how much more of this she could take. Her diagnostic instincts were spot on and almost always validated by tests, which was one reason she'd gone into emergency medicine. But these long shifts, especially the night shift, got old. Especially when people didn't do what they were told.

"Got a new one for you, doc," said Stan, the charge nurse. He leaned over the counter extending a clipboard. With a glance at her weary feet, Grace slipped her shoes back on, stood, and straightened the white jacket over her blue scrubs. "Urgent?"

"Not so much. Probably a bad ankle sprain. 'Mr. Hottie' thought it might be more, so he stopped by to have it checked out."

Her eyebrow shot up. "Mr. Hottie?"

"Why do you think it's so quiet here. Everyone's checking out McDreamy-who-isn't-a-doctor, and he's holding court."

Great. Exactly what she needed. Some arrogant jerk who thought he ruled the world. Grace rubbed her forehead with her palm. When she'd accepted the job at this small Aberdeen hospital, she'd figured a smaller city would mean less trouble in the ER. Except, not so much. She'd traded big city fights, guns, and drugs for a smaller community's drama and eccentricities. Now, she was confronted by a whole new set of problems and didn't have a handle on them yet. Which was why every shift left her exhausted. And that had nothing to do with the fact that Christmas, when it always got harder to keep the memories from overwhelming her, was less than a month away.

"Send him for X-rays, then I'll check on him."

"You know that's not how we work here. Doctor's eyes on the patient, then tests."

Another small-town idiosyncrasy. In Chicago, there wasn't time for doctors to babysit patients. Triage nurses ordered basic tests, then the physician stepped in.

"Fine," she said, grabbing the clipboard. She strode down the hall to room eight. Even given what Stan had told her, she was surprised to see a group of women milling around outside the room. Rolling her eyes, she shooed them off to go about their business. She knew they called her Dr. Ice. She didn't care. She wasn't here to make friends. She had a job to do.

Rounding the corner into the room, two things struck Grace simultaneously. First, the room was more crowded than it should have been for an ankle injury, even if the foot sticking out from beneath the sheet looked rather large and well-groomed. Second, the other side of the sheet was folded below a snug, long-sleeved t-shirt with *Jones Snowboards* emblazoned across the front of a well-muscled chest.

But the thing that struck her the most was the wide, relaxed grin on the man's face as he chatted with the women around him. He should be in pain. Instead, he acted comfortable and in his element. His dark hair and beard offset the lighter brown of his eyes and very white teeth. Pulled in by the man's demeanor, a subtle extra thump or two in the vicinity of her heart made her place a hand there for a moment. What had that been? The beginning of another panic attack? She hadn't had one of those since leaving Chicago, so why now? She grew irritated as she took deep breaths to stave off the feeling that she'd lost control of a situation before she'd even assessed it.

Why was he so happy? If he wasn't in pain, why had he come to her ER? Control, that's what she needed. Control and organization put everything in perspective and kept her world orderly and neat, exactly how she liked it.

"All right, break is over," she said to the bevy of women standing around the patient's bed. "Time to get back to work."

They filed past her, some quite reluctantly and with heavy sighs.

Grace had the patient's full attention now and she almost took a step back. The man's gaze held hers with a focus she'd never experienced before, like she'd become his whole world and nothing else mattered. He angled his head as he looked her over. The grin returned and it was oh, so cocky.

"You must be the doctor," he said in a voice that thrummed through her like the smooth bass of jazz music.

Though she considered giving him props for not calling her the nurse, Grace knew if she gave him anything, he'd take a mile. Part of her wanted to let him. Something about him resonated deep inside her and set her body to humming. Damn it. She needed to control this situation. Control herself.

The man watched her, waiting for her to answer. What had he asked? Oh, yes. Who she was.

"I'm Dr. Benson," she said, flipping a page on the clipboard and reading it. "Name and birthdate, please? Hospital rules say I have to confirm."

"Anytime, doctor. Name's Cade Huntington." He added his birthdate, which Grace barely heard, she got so pulled in by his voice. This would not do at all.

"Ankle injury?"

He nodded, still grinning.

"How did you hurt it?"

"Snowboarding. Took a mogul too fast and had to correct—"

As he used his arms to show the movement of his board, Grace followed the curves of those long-fingered hands, mesmerized.

"Didn't see the second mogul and it took me down. So, do you have a first name, doctor?"

"I do," she answered, grateful her badge was turned around. No way was she giving this man any information. Something about him screamed danger and she sure as hell didn't need that in her life.

She pulled the sheet up to look at the red and swollen ankle, trying to ignore the well-muscled leg it was attached to. Experience said the ankle was a sprain, but while Grace trusted her instincts, she believed in facts.

"We'll get a few X-rays and see what's up."

He smiled at her and she realized she envied the ease of his interactions with people. For her, chatting with strangers didn't come easy.

"Thank you, Dr. Benson."

With a nod, she left the room, wrote the orders, and turned the clipboard over to Stan. Then she fled to the restroom. Inside the stall, she sank down and tried to figure out what had gotten into her. Why would she react like this to some random guy? An ER patient, no less. This had never happened before. Maybe she was coming down with something. Grace felt her forehead. No fever that she could tell. Still, she was sweaty, her heart raced, and her brain was all fuzzy. Why?

Could it be simply because he's attractive?

No. Grace tossed the idea aside like the Brussels sprouts she refused to eat. She didn't do attraction. The one or two times she had, nothing good had come of it. Grace stood and straightened her scrubs. Relationships were not her forte. She recognized that and accepted it. She knew how to run her life, and how not to.

She could deal with Mr. Hottie. He'd be out of her ER in an hour. She could finish her shift and go home to her orderly house and slip into her bed for some much-needed sleep. Outside the stall, she washed her hands and nodded emphatically at herself in the mirror. She had a plan and life was good.

Half an hour later, she stood outside Cade Huntington's room chewing her lip, struggling to take the steps to get him out of her hospital.

After giving herself a firm talking-to, she entered with brisk efficiency to find four hospital employees— all women—had once again migrated to Mr. Hottie's side. Grace stared at them all until they mumbled excuses and slid past her back to work.

"Dr. Grace. I've been waiting for you to come back." His husky voice almost made her fail to notice his use of her first name.

Grace narrowed her eyes, which only made him grin wider. Arrogant and self-assured. Something she would never be and never wanted to be around.

"Your X-rays don't show any fracture, so this," she pointed to his ankle, "is most likely a bad sprain."

"Just as I thought. Will you have dinner with me?"

"What?"

"Dinner. You know. Food? You do eat, don't you, Dr. Grace?"

"I— I— " Grace took a couple deep breaths. Although she was used to flirtatious patients, it irritated her that *he* was flirting with her. "Mr. Huntington, that is not proper. You will refer to me as Dr. Benson. And no, I will not have dinner with you. I don't date patients."

"Good to know you date someone. The rest, we'll have to figure out as we go."

She really needed to regain control of this situation. "Mr. Huntington, we're going to put you in a boot and send you home. The sprain is pretty bad, so you'll need to stay off that ankle—no weight bearing at all—for at least a week to give it time to heal. We can give you crutches."

"I won't need the crutches," he said, the grin never leaving his face.

"You can't be non-weight bearing without them."

He didn't respond, just held her eyes captive with his own. Grace wanted to fall into them, to smooth the unruly waves in his dark hair, to taste the lips that smiled so readily.

Damn it. No. She was not falling for some snake whisperer's charms. "I'll get your orders written up and you'll be out of here within the hour. Do you need any pain medication?"

"No. I can take ibuprofen. I prefer not to take anything stronger."

"Good." She turned, intent on getting the hell out of the room.

"Dr. Grace?"

Double damn it. She couldn't just ignore him, so she turned back. "Yes?"

"I will convince you to go out with me. I want to make sure you know that."

Her face felt like it was in flames. She whirled and fled as quickly as protocols allowed. Once she'd found Stan, she shoved the clipboard with her final orders at him, then went to the lounge for ER personnel, empty at this time of night, thankfully. Whatever that had been, whoever Cade Huntington was, she wouldn't have to see him again. Her nice, orderly world would remain as it was.

So why didn't that thought, normally calming, settle her now?

No new patients came in for the next while, so Grace remained in the break room for a solid forty minutes. Figuring the coast had to be clear, she headed back to the nurse's station. A few hours remained in her shift and she wasn't one to shirk her duties.

As she rounded the corner, she glimpsed the waiting room. Cade Huntington was limping his way to the exit, one foot in a boot, and carrying his crutches. Damn it. He should listen to her. She knew what she was talking about. If he didn't stay off that ankle, he'd have worse problems to come.

As the door swooshed open automatically, he stopped and turned, his gaze finding her. With a smile, he waved his crutches at her and limped out the door. And out of her life.

Thank God.

~~~

Never in his life had Cade reacted to a woman so strongly. This time of night, the clinic his parents ran in Willow Bay was closed. Plus, he wouldn't have gone there anyway, where he'd have to their rants about his life. Cade shook his head. He didn't need that kind of grief. So he'd driven to the closest hospital, Grays Harbor General, and encountered a different type of complication.

Meeting that doctor had thrown him for a loop. Dr. Grace. What was it about the winsome physician that strummed the right chord? She was beautiful. No arguing that, with her blonde hair and those intelligent blue eyes. She was also very uptight, something he didn't generally go for in a woman. He'd accepted an unrequested challenge and told her he would convince her to go out with him.

What the hell had gotten into him? Especially added to that parting shot, walking out without using his crutches. Now his ankle hurt like a son of a bitch. He climbed into his SUV and gulped down four ibuprofen without water, then laid his head against the headrest and breathed in and out, wishing the pain away.

Not that it worked. The ankle throbbed like crazy and he had a forty-minute drive home. As it turned out, an agonizing forty-five-minute drive. When Cade hit the button to open his garage door and pulled in, it was after 2 a.m. and all he wanted to do was sink into bed. And get his damn ankle above his heart. He remembered that much from the doctor's advice.

Actually, he remembered everything. Every nuance of her silky voice, the wariness in her eyes, his desire to pull the pins out of her bun and see how long and luxurious those blonde tresses really were. He hadn't been that into a woman since... Well, it had been a long time.

Using the damn crutches, Cade walked through his house without turning on the lights. He didn't need to thanks to the Christmas lights he'd put up everywhere. He grabbed an ice pack and a bottle of water from the fridge, then climbed the stairs to his bedroom, tripping on the fourth stair and going down.

"Damn crutches." Cade did the rest of the stairs on his butt, cussing the whole way. At the top, he threw the crutches down and hopped into his room. He wasn't unfamiliar with crutches, but it had been a while and he hated them now as much as he did then.

The ibuprofen had finally taken the edge off. Shedding his clothes, he sank into his mattress, wrapped an ice pack around the ankle, and put it up on a pillow. Drinking water could wait. Right now, he needed sleep and healing.

Except neither came easy. He couldn't stop thinking about threading his fingers through long, blonde locks, staring into the deep blue eyes that haunted him, coaxing a smile from those lips that were born to be kissed.

Chapter Two

Her shift over—finally—Grace slipped into her leather-seated SUV and turned on some jazz for her drive home. She worked in Grays Harbor's biggest town, but the ocean had called her, so she'd bought a little house in Willow Bay. The drive was only about half an hour and quiet, especially in the early light. The world was just waking up as she headed home for some much-needed sleep. Strains of Kenny G lulled her into a reflective mood as she thought about her shift. Her night had been blessedly quiet after Mr. Hottie left, though it still galled her that he'd thrown her advice in the toilet and walked out putting weight on that ankle. What was it about people, men especially, that made them fail to listen to solid advice? She knew her stuff and was getting pretty damn tired of folks ignoring her instructions.

Thankfully, the police had found the dementia patient. He would be spending a couple days in the hospital to get him straightened out. And to find him some pants.

In all honesty, people usually did listen to her. This shift had just been fraught with the unmindful kind of patient. Christmas did that to people. With so much to do, they had no choice but to be selfish with their time and their brainpower. Yet another reason to happily naysay the season. Even thinking about it brought a quick stab of pain to her heart, so Grace shoved those thoughts far, far away.

Not so easy to do as she drove through Willow Bay with all its festive lights and greenery on bright display. She hadn't known Willow Bay went big for Christmas when she'd moved here three months earlier. It might have swayed her opinion of the cute little town. But she was here now, so she'd deal.

At least she wouldn't have to interact with Cade Huntington again. Or so she hoped. His chart listed a Willow Bay address, but it was on the opposite side of town to her place and she'd never seen him around. That gave her confidence that he was out of her life. Last night had been quite enough of the brash, arrogant man. Even as she thought this, a vague sense of disloyalty stung her heart, because somehow, he'd peeled back the outer layers of her defenses the moment she'd met him. Damn traitorous libido. She'd met nice-looking men before, so why had he affected her? His attitude was the antithesis of what she looked for in a man. She wanted someone who cared about business, organization, knowledge. Not some happy-go-lucky guy with a smile that could melt glaciers.

Besides, he'd completely disregarded her orders to stay off that ankle. That galled her. Nothing she could do about it now except let it go. Not an easy thing to do, apparently. Thoughts of this man would crowd into her brain the moment she let her guard down. It was irritating.

Driving down the main street of Willow Bay, the only person Grace saw this morning was a bundled-up figure pushing a rickety shopping cart. And headed away from the shelter. Why was she moving in that direction?

Why was she wandering around at the crack of dawn and so hunched over? Was she in crisis? Confused? Grace punched the phone button on her steering wheel.

"Call the Willow Bay Sheriff non-emergency number."

Within seconds, a deep voice answered. "Willow Bay Sheriff's office, Officer Smith speaking."

"Hello officer, my name is Dr. Grace Benson. I'm on my way home from a shift at Grays Harbor General and I saw a street person who could be in trouble. I wasn't sure if I should call it in or not, so tried the non-emergency number."

"You did just fine. Can you tell me what the person looked like?"

"Not too well. The person was bundled up. I couldn't even say if it was a man or a woman. They were pushing a rickety old shopping cart piled high and covered with a tarp."

The chuckle on the other end of the line confused Grace. "Did I say something funny?" she said in her most imperious tone. Granted, she'd never really gotten the hang of humor.

"Sorry," the officer said. "To ease your concerns, I know who you saw. That would be Gladys, our resident, stubborn street person, and a friend to most of the town that she considers her own. She tries to run it, at any rate."

Her own town? "A street person tries to run Willow Bay?"

Another chuckle. "You must be new here." His deep, sonorous voice calmed Grace's pique somewhat.

"I bought a place three months ago."

"Oh, you may have bought the little place next to me and Aimi. I'm Jackson Smith. Aimi Larson is my fiancé and the town's attorney."

"I've seen her rushing out to her car."

"Yes." He chuckled again. "I've been tasked with figuring out how to get her an attached garage. She's not much of a rain person."

And Willow Bay got a lot of rain. Grace smiled, letting the rest of her irritation go. "So this Gladys is not ill or infirm, then?"

"I think she's fine. It's not unusual to see her at this time."

"Why doesn't she stay in the shelter?"

"No one knows. She accepts food from the various restaurants, but won't take handouts for places to stay. Says she's got her haunt and she's content there."

Unusual, to say the least. "Well, if this is a non-issue, I'm going home to get some sleep."

"Have a good day, er, night, Dr. Benson."

Grace punched the end button just as she parked in front of her nice, neat little house and yard, still wondering about the street person. Why would someone refuse a place to stay? Especially in a town where she seemed comfortable?

Oh well, not her problem. Grace stretched her neck and shoulders, trying to let it go. She grabbed her bag, shut off her alarm, and went inside her nice, orderly home. Coming home always calmed her. She loved the one-hundred-year-old house, even with its quirks. The dark molding offset by newly painted white walls looked almost Bavarian. Grace set her bag down on the metal and wood cart island she'd found at a little antique shop a couple towns over.

She heard a thump and a familiar warble.

"Hello, Luna," Grace said, crouching down to pick up her gray tabby cat and give her some love. She hugged her close, Luna's purrs unwinding the tension in Grace's shoulders even more. "Did you have a good night?"

Luna had been her loyal companion all through medical school and residency. The move here from

Chicago had traumatized the ten-year-old feline. It had taken over a week for her to leave her crate for more than food and water. Once she'd finally begun to explore, she'd settled into her new digs. An indoor-only cat, Luna seemed completely content now with her life in Willow Bay. Her favorite place, if she wasn't on Grace's lap, was the bay window where she watched the ebb and flow of the sleepy world outside.

With a deep yawn, Grace set Luna down, fed her, and made herself some oatmeal. After that, it was past time for sleep. She headed upstairs with her faithful companion plodding along behind, ready to put last night out of her mind.

Chapter Three

"Damn crutches," Cade muttered as he got out of his SUV. He'd throw the crutches away, but he'd just spent the day on the couch and was about maxed out on ibuprofen, mostly due to his little stunt last night. Lesson learned. And as much as he preferred his own cooking to a restaurant, standing in the kitchen for the time necessary to make a good meal didn't sound fun, either.

He locked the SUV and hobbled toward the entrance to Pacific Lodge, Willow Bay's most exclusive digs and the most upscale restaurant in town. He didn't mind a good burger and fries but was in the mood for something more than that, so here he was.

"Cade," the pretty blonde manager said, hugging him as he walked in the door. "What happened?"

"Hi, Joey. Just a sprain, no biggee." He tapped the floor with his boot and squirmed at the bolt of pain.

"Looks like more than that. What brings you out tonight?"

"Didn't feel like cooking." Joey was cute and vivacious and acted much younger than her thirty-five years. Older or not, Cade had been tempted to ask her out, but they'd become friends since she'd settled here and it was comfortable. She was like the older sister he'd never had.

"Your timing's good. The restaurant isn't very full. And you'll like the chef's special tonight."

"Please say it's seafood."

She smiled. "It is."

When Cade stumbled taking a step toward the restaurant, Joey put a hand out to steady him. "Do you need some help getting there?"

Oh, please. The day he needed help with a sprained ankle was the day he bought a wheelchair and gave up on life. He glanced at Joey, seeing the laughter twinkling in her eyes. "Good thing you're joking, woman."

"All right, go enjoy your dinner. And be careful not to fall. We don't need any more liability issues here."

Any more? Before Cade could ask, she'd turned away to help someone else so Cade crutched his way into the restaurant. The first people he saw were Luke and Jasmin Taylor, so he stopped at their table.

"How are the newlyweds?" They'd sprung a surprise wedding on everyone the night of Aimi and Jackson's engagement party. It was chaotic and awesome and Cade couldn't be happier for them, even if Jasmin had turned him down in favor of Luke. Clearly, these two were destined for each other.

"Loving every minute of it," Luke said. He put an arm around his wife as she blushed.

Cade laughed. "I bet."

"Been skiing again?" Luke asked, pointing to his gimped-up leg.

Cade nodded. "Took a mogul wrong."

"Ouch. Want to join us?" Jasmin said. "We've only just put our order in."

Having taken a moment to glance around the restaurant, Cade noticed someone else he knew. Sort of. Tonight was looking better and better. "Actually, I see someone I know, so maybe we can dine together another day? I'd love to have you over to the house for dinner."

Jasmin glanced where Cade's gaze had gone and smiled. "That would be great."

"All right then. Enjoy your dinner."

"You too," they said, though Jasmin's words were tinged with laughter.

Cade barely heard them. He navigated the tables like a man on a mission until his crutch caught the leg of a chair. He went down like Mario falling off a sky block, landing with an oomph right beside Dr. Grace Benson's chair.

He lay there catching his breath. He looked up straight into angelic green eyes full of turmoil. He almost laughed at himself, but that hint of worry was something he couldn't quite figure out.

"Are you alright?" she said, leaning down.

"If I said I needed mouth-to-mouth, would you believe me?" He put his best earnest face on. When she sat back and pressed her lips together, Cade picked himself up, along with his battered pride, and settled into the chair opposite her.

"Mind if I join you?" he asked.

Her mouth opened, then closed. "You already have, it seems."

Hmmm. Women usually didn't react to him in an adversarial way. Though he wanted to get to know Dr. Grace, if she didn't want that, well, he would respect her wishes. As much as it disappointed him to do so, he stood and reached for his crutches. "I'm sorry to have bothered you."

"Oh, sit down, before you fall down again."

He did, happy that he'd been given a reprieve.

"Seriously, are you alright?"

"After a little fall like that?"

Man, when Dr. Grace stared someone down, she

really stared them down. She didn't blink or waver and the consternation in her furrowed brow didn't relent. For the first time in his life, Cade felt intimidated. Also, for the first time in his life, he wanted more of this woman.

"Yes. Seriously. I'm okay," he finally answered. "It's mostly my pride that got wounded."

She nodded, her expression relaxing.

The waiter joined them, and Grace held her menu out to Cade, who waved it off. "Thank you, but I know what I want." He gestured for her to order.

"I'll have the special," she said. Nice that she spared a smile for the waiter but not him. And that she didn't ask for any substitutions or changes to the chef's choice for the day.

"I'll have the same."

"Anything to drink?" the waiter asked.

"Water," they said at the same time, and both smiled.

Wow. When Dr. Grace smiled, the world brightened. Dimples peeked out. This woman had so many facets, and Cade wanted to get to know every single one.

Her smile faded after the waiter left, replaced by a slight stern frown. Cade opted for honesty. "Did I do something to offend you?"

"You mean like walking out of the ER putting your full weight on that ankle?" She sat up straighter with each word.

Cade felt the heat crawl up his neck. Yeah, he'd gone overboard with that. She had every right to berate him. "That was me being manly, though it backfired big time. Turns out, you were right. Putting weight on the ankle only made it worse. If it makes you feel any better, I've spent all day flat on my back with the leg on pillows, icing and eating ibuprofen like candy. I only just started recovering from that stupid stunt before I came here."

"I'm sorry," Grace said, her voice softening. "That's a tough way to learn a lesson."

The concern in her eyes almost did Cade in. He wanted to sink into them and get lost. Which, he realized, he very well might do, and he wasn't at all ready for that. Still, dinner with a beautiful woman was much better than a solo burger at home, even if he did make a pretty awesome burger.

"Thank you for letting me stay and have dinner with you."

"You didn't give me much of a choice."

Oh, yeah, he was totally getting off on the wrong foot, er, ankle. "I apologize for that, too. I'm happy to move to another table."

"Stay. Please."

Had he caught a hint of regret?

"You're here now. And company might be nice."

"Thank you. Dinner with such a beautiful and impressive woman will make my day." He meant it. Her blonde hair, down tonight so he could see that it fell halfway to her waist, had soft waves like wheat undulating beneath a gentle breeze. Her eyes seemed to change color with her mood. Green now. Cade hoped that equaled contentedness. She sat tall in her chair and when someone spoke, they got all her focus. He'd bet anything she was a good listener.

"Flattery will not get you anywhere," Grace said, her voice quiet but still commanding. She was used to being in charge.

Cade cocked his head. "Not flattery. Don't you know how stunning you look? Or how smart you are? And for you to invite me to stay when I did nothing to earn it? I barely know you but I think you're an amazing woman, Dr. Grace. That's not flattery. It's a compliment."

Grace's mouth formed a small "o" as she listened to

him. She seemed completely unaware of the effect she had on men and Cade wondered how that could be. At the same time, he loved the lack of self-importance she projected. Unlike him, who pushed his way to the front on a regular basis. He could learn a lot from this lady. For now, he'd settle for getting to know her a little bit.

"So, how did you come to be an ER physician at Grays Harbor?" he asked.

~~~

Grace was about as discombobulated as she'd ever been in her life. Cade Huntington could turn her world upside down with one kind word. No one had ever complimented her like that before except her father. The man barely knew her. How could he believe those nice things about her?

"Grace?" Cade covered her hand with his. She slid her hand out from beneath his and onto her lap, rubbing the warmth she felt from his touch.

"I don't know you well enough to hold hands." She took a sip of water. "What did you ask?"

"I asked how you came to work in the area."

"I finished residency back in Chicago and decided I didn't want to work in an inner-city hospital. I searched for smaller communities and this job turned up." This was foreign territory, talking about herself.

"Chicago, eh? I was there once, for a convention. In winter. They can be brutal."

"Yes."

"How long have you been out here, then?"

"Not long."

"And you live in Willow Bay?"

"Maybe." She cocked her head at him.

Cade grinned. "You don't like talking about yourself, do you?"

"Astute man."

Cade spread his arms wide. "That's me. Astute,

good-looking, and interested in what makes beautiful women like yourself tick."

In any other man, that comment would be sexist and chauvinistic. In Cade Huntington, it was disarming. Grace needed to watch herself with him. He could charm secrets out of a cobra.

"There's really not much to talk about. I led a boring life, stuck my head in a book until I got through medical school, and here I am."

"Oh, I think you're more complex than that, Dr. Grace. I've never looked forward to getting to know a woman so much. Not even close."

The fierce heat of a blush, the only thing she couldn't control, rose up her neck. Point to Cade Huntington. And Grace didn't give points graciously. It was time to regain control of this situation. History had taught her that losing control meant she'd be the one hurt.

Thankfully, their dinner arrived, and the chef's take on shrimp scampi looked delicious. Grace took a bite and savored the flavors as they melted in her mouth. This was heaven. Grace took a second bite before she looked up to see Cade staring at her, fork in hand. It didn't look like he'd taken a single bite.

"Don't you like the dish?" she asked.

"I love their scampi. I've had it before. I was just taking a moment to enjoy your reaction. I take it Pacific Lodge food is new to you?"

"This is absolutely delicious. And yes, it's the first time I've eaten here."

"Then we'll have to come back. Chef does some amazing things with food. So, do you mostly cook at home?"

Come back? With Cade? While the idea reached out to her in unexpected ways, it couldn't happen. Better to stay focused on the here and now and let this surge of feeling go at the end of the evening. Food. Stay focused on food. That was safe. "No. I don't generally cook, especially not during my work week."

"I've heard ER docs work twelve-hour shifts."

Grace nodded, chewing another delicious, aromatic bite.

"So what do you eat?"

She shrugged. "Hospital cafeteria food, mostly. I try to eat well on my days off. This really is good. You should eat before it gets cold."

Cade's grin froze Grace in time as she basked in its easy charm.

"I'm not going to disobey doctor's orders again." He took a bite of shrimp and looked up at the ceiling as he chewed, savoring the taste. Cade didn't seem to do anything halfway. He was all in or nothing, whereas Grace preferred measured dedication. If you got too involved, or you felt too strongly, it only led to pain.

The next few minutes were spent eating quietly as they both enjoyed their dinner.

"You should let me cook for you one of these days. I'm pretty good in the kitchen, though this—" he tapped the boot on his left foot— "puts a crimp in my skills."

"I don't think that's a good idea," Grace said. She did not need to get involved with this handsome man. Cade was a complication and Grace didn't do those. Ever.

"Why not?"

How could she answer that question? "I'm not into dating right now. I'm completely focused on settling into the new job and getting my house fixed up the way I'd like it." Hopefully, that would satisfy his curiosity.

"Do you need some help with your house? I'm pretty handy."

"No. I've got it handled. What kind of work do you do?" she asked, quickly changing the subject.

The look on Cade's face said he knew her intent, but he bit anyhow. "I, um, install cable systems and internet in homes and businesses around the area." He paused, almost as if he wanted to say more. Instead he asked her if she had cable.

"I don't own a television and I went with satellite for my internet."

Cade's eyes widened. "I don't think I've ever met someone who doesn't have a TV."

"I have books. And music."

"What kind of music do you like?" He put an elbow on the table beside his now empty plate, and his chin in his palm, as if settling in for a nice, long, chat. Grace wasn't interested.

"Is your whole family as inquisitive as you? My gosh, you must have been precocious as a two-year-old."

"I'm an only child." Cade stiffened and sat up. Something about his family life bugged him, and that intrigued Grace. Family dynamics, something she hadn't had much of in her life, interested her. She wanted to understand what normal family life was like.

"I guess you're right. I ask too many questions." Cade said, waving for the waiter to bring the bill. "Anyway, I've overstayed my welcome."

When the waiter set the bill down, Cade reached for it.

"Where's my bill?" Grace asked.

"I've got this," he said.

"No. I pay my own way."

"Look, I horned in on your evening. It's only fair." He plunked several twenties down on the table and stood. "I hope to see you around Willow Bay, Dr. Grace. I'd like to spend some time with you. Give it some thought and let me know if that interests you. This is my cell number." Cade handed her a card with the local cable company's logo and held her fingers a moment longer than propriety dictated. Then, with a tip of his imaginary hat and a quick smile, he grabbed his crutches and hobbled out. Carefully this time.

And thankfully, not putting weight on the sprained ankle. Grace smiled as she watched him leave, then noticed the couple he'd spoken to on his way in. They watched her with avid interest and she looked away, unwilling to give this small town anything to gossip about.

In the lodge foyer, she found Cade waiting for her.

"I'm sorry I left so abruptly. I—I don't get along well with my folks, so it's not something I talk about. I guess I didn't know how to answer your question."

His candor slithered right through her defenses. "I appreciate the honesty, Cade. That's important to me."

He smiled, this time more circumspectly and with less abandon. Grace found she missed his all-in smile. They walked outside together.

"Would you like to take a walk on the beach with me?" Cade asked.

Grace looked at him like he was nuts. "It's dark out. And December. And you're on crutches."

"The moon's full and the beach is pretty this time of year, with all that light shining on the water. If we stick to the hard-packed sand, I'll be fine on the crutches. Besides, you look nice and bundled up." He reached for the collar of her coat and snugged it tighter around her neck, his hand resting on her shoulder for a few seconds.

"I'm sorry, I don't do cold well. Maybe some other time."

"Are you working this week?"

"Not until Friday." Now why had she given him that information?

He gave a quick nod, then hobbled with her to her car, opening the door after she unlocked it with her fob. "Chef does a great prime rib on Thursdays. Interested in coming back with me to try it?"

Prime rib was her favorite meal in the whole wide world. With an unfettered regret, she declined. "I'm not sure that's a great idea, Cade. Like I said, I need to focus on other things right now."

"All right." He held the door as she climbed in. "Just to be clear, Dr. Grace, I'm interested in getting to know you better. If not now, then whenever you will let me. You've got my card. I hope you call."

With one more award-winning smile, he quietly shut her door and turned, heading over to a nice-looking SUV. He got in but didn't pull out, so Grace started her car and drove to the parking lot exit. When Cade pulled up behind her, she wondered if he would try to follow her. How did the cable guy manage to own a Lexus, and a nice one, from what she could tell? Nervous, wondering if he was the kind of guy to push the issue, she turned left toward home, breathing much easier when he turned right. Reflecting on how pleasant—and how confusing—the night had been, she almost didn't see the person crossing the street with a cart.

Grace slammed on her brakes as Gladys whipped her cart around to shield herself from the oncoming car. They stopped mere inches from each other. Grace was out of her car and around the cart in an instant.

"Are you all right? I'm so sorry. I didn't see you in the dark."

"I'm fine," the old woman said. "Never touched me and I'm quick to react." She leaned forward and peered into Grace's eyes. "Was it just the dark or were you thinking about someone so hard you got distracted?"

Thinking about someone? Where did this woman get that idea? Never mind that Grace *had* been doing that exact thing.

"You're sure you're all right, then? I'm a doctor so if anything's bothering you, we should check it out."

"Oh, no dearie. I'm just fine, but I appreciate the offer."

"You're Gladys, right? The sheriff mentioned your name."

"That's me. Guessin' the whole town knows me by now. You must be new here. And a doctor, too, huh? Willow Bay could use more of them. The ones that own the clinic have to be close to retiring."

Grace had considered the clinic Gladys was talking about. They'd advertised for doctors, but she'd opted to stay in the hospital setting. Reaching into her coat, Grace pulled out a business card with her cell number on it. She handed it to Gladys. "The sheriff says you're good people, Gladys. I work at Grays Harbor General Hospital. If you ever need any medical help, you give me a call."

"That is very sweet of you." Gladys looked down at the card then back up at Grace. "Dr. Benson. I'll keep that in mind."

"Do you want a ride to, you know, wherever you're going?"

"Oh, no, dearie. Thank you, but Mabel here"—she patted her stuffed cart—"would never fit in your car. I'll be just fine. I'm about home, anyhow."

"Oh? Where's home?"

Gladys looked like she knew she'd let something slip. She covered it up by tucking Grace's card into her pocket and grabbing hold of her cart. "Oh, here, there, wherever I want it to be. Have a good rest of your evening, Dr. Benson. And thank you for checking on me."

Grace watched as Gladys walked away. What an enigma. The woman spoke like a cultured person, but added words like dearie, almost as if she was trying to mislead people into thinking she wasn't educated. She was a mystery and Grace had always been drawn to those. Most of the fiction she read was mystery.

Back in her car, Grace resumed her drive home with a completely different set of problems on her mind.

Chapter Four

At nine the next morning, Cade sat outside Grace's house. Technically, he sat outside Jackson and Aimi's house. When they'd mentioned the new tenant next door was a doctor, Cade had realized who it had to be. Now he sat in his truck thinking about knocking on her door and wondering if he could be accused of stalking. He hadn't been able to stop thinking about her all the sleep-deprived night and knew, if he left it in her hands to call him, she might never do that. Her place was small and cute. It needed a paint job, but that was a never-ending job near the ocean. The windows were new and black vinyl, so trendy. He'd bet anything she'd gone modern inside. She also lived right next to the sheriff. He wondered if she'd met Jackson and Aimi yet. Both were nice people.

Now here he sat, unsure of himself, a rarity for him. He found Grace mesmerizing and completely honest and disarming. Sure, she was a bit stiff, but he'd bet anything hot blood raced beneath that hard shell. He wanted to break through that tough exterior and learn about the woman beneath the façade.

He wouldn't be able to do that sitting here in his

truck, so Cade got out and crutched his way up to her front door like he knew what he was doing, which he didn't. He rapped three times. If it worked for that Sheldon geek on the television show, maybe it would work for him?

She opened the door, dressed and with makeup on as if ready to head out the door. Shoot, maybe she had plans. Her eyes widened when she saw him.

"Hi," he said lamely, leaning on one crutch.

"Cade? What the— How— What are you doing here?" She let go of the door and reached down to pick up a large gray cat. Another piece of information about Dr. Grace. She liked cats.

He shrugged, knowing he had no excuse. "I didn't want to wait to see you again."

Her hand stroked the cat, who watched him with shuttered eyes. Cade reached out to the animal, who immediately stiffened. Grace's eyes became small slits as she stared at him.

"You don't know where I live. I mean, you shouldn't. Did you follow me home last night?"

He pulled his hand back, stuffing it in his pocket. "God, no. I'm not a stalker." He winced inwardly. "Never been before, at any rate." He'd better come clean. He pointed to Jackson and Aimi's. "Had to fix their cable and Jackson mentioned a doctor had moved in next door. I took a chance."

Her eyes narrowed. "That doesn't sound exactly plausible."

"It's not. It's…fate." Cade grinned. "Shit. Does that make me a stalker?" Cade ran a hand through his hair.

Grace shivered.

"You're cold," he said.

"Yes, I am." She looked down the street, then back at him, one lovely eyebrow arched. That wasn't a good sign. Shaking her head, Grace opened the door wider.

"You're here. You might as well come in."

"Thanks," he said, flashing his smile as he maneuvered carefully past the cat still giving him the stink eye from her owner's arms. So far, so good. He looked around, realizing he'd been completely wrong on her choice of décor as he took in the dark wood edges and doors and white walls. Even her furniture was more comfortable than stylish. Another facet.

"Don't get any ideas. You and I both know who I live next door to." She set the cat down and Cade had an anxious moment as the fur ball strutted straight for him. The sheriff wasn't the only scary thing around here.

"Not planning to try anything. And for reference, Jackson usually has Mondays and Tuesdays off. He works most of the weekend shifts." The cat had reached Cade and sniffed his shoes.

"You two friends?"

"Me and the cat? Uh, no."

Grace bit back a smile. "You and the sheriff."

"Everyone in Willow Bay is a friend."

"I'm learning that the hard way, it seems."

The cat decided Cade was either safe or boring. It sat back on its haunches and proceeded to clean itself. "What's your cat's name?"

"Luna. Why are you here, Cade?"

He wanted to step forward, to touch her. Run his hands over her lips. Instead, he tightened his hold on his crutch. Her gaze followed the movement, then abruptly returned to his face. The telltale pinkening of her cheeks told him she wasn't completely unaffected by his presence.

"I wondered if you'd like to come clamming with me."

"Today? It's, what, forty degrees out?"

"Balmy for December. And no rain expected for hours. Clamming's good on days like this."

"And you thought I was nuts for living in Chicago?"

"Point taken." He laughed. "However, if you bundle up, the beach can be nice this time of year. It's good for the soul, and we certainly won't be the only ones out there."

"You're on crutches."

Cade shrugged. "I think I can get around on the beach all right. And not bear weight on the bad ankle. I try very hard not to let injuries like this keep me from doing things, but I'm being mindful."

The skepticism on her face said he hadn't yet convinced her. "I'll buy you hot chocolate afterward."

There it was, a softening in her eyes, a crinkle starting to form at the edges. "I do like hot chocolate."

"And I know the perfect place to get some."

"I don't know, Cade. You and me? Not a good idea."

"You keep saying that, but I don't get it. Besides, this is clamming and hot chocolate. I'm not inviting myself to your bedroom."

They both paused at that, Cade fighting the strong desire to look up toward the second floor of her house and Grace's blush deepening.

"I promise, I'll be a perfect gentleman." *Whether I want to or not. Sigh.*

"I need a few minutes to change."

"I've got time. Do you have rubber boots?"

"No. Just snow boots."

"I've got a pair in the SUV that might fit you. I'll go get them while you change."

Grace nodded, then headed for the stairs. Cade made it to the Lexus and back in record time, crutches or not, afraid to give her a chance to lock the door behind him.

When she came downstairs a few minutes later, she'd changed into sweat pants that clung to her hips and thighs. She had at least two layers of shirts on and a jean shirt over them.

"See if these fit you," Cade said, handing over the boots. They did, so she grabbed coat, hat, and purse, and they were out the door.

"Wait, I don't have any clam digging stuff. Honestly, I don't even know what I need."

"I have enough for both of us." He held out his hand and held his breath.

She paused, gazing at his hand for a moment. She set her gloved one in his, just for a moment, then pulled away. In that brief span, Cade's world fell into place and there was nowhere else he wanted to be except right here, right now, with Grace. He held the door open as she climbed in the SUV, then whistled as he limped around to his door.

"Wow, pretty ritzy wheels here," Grace said. "That cable gig of yours must pay well for you to afford this."

He turned on the seat warmers. "That and some other stuff I've got going on. Come on. Let's hit the beach."

Dating wasn't something Grace did. Well, at least not very often. She also rarely warmed up to people, especially those who didn't listen to her. So why had she accepted Cade's invitation? And his hand. Because she'd wanted to, more than anything she'd wanted in a while, except maybe getting out of Chicago or getting a new childhood. Maybe giving someone else a little control wouldn't hurt? She didn't know anything about clamming but loved clams. This was a perfect opportunity to learn.

Cade drove with the same kind of assurance with which he seemed to live his life. Soon, they turned onto the beach road. When he didn't stop and drove right onto the beach, Grace grabbed the armrest, causing him to glance at her.

"The best place to dig clams is about half a mile up. You've never driven on the beach?"

"No. I haven't come down here much."

"How come?"

He didn't censure or berate her. Grace liked that.

"At first, I was house-hunting and settling into the job and the drive. Then I was doing minor renovations, and still settling into the job. Then the weather tanked." She watched the waves roll in, so majestic in their rush to steal sand from the shoreline.

"Is the tide coming in or going out?" she asked.

"It's almost low tide, which means the clam beds are exposed and we'll have some slack tide time to dig them up."

"There's a lot of beach here."

"You should see it at high tide. Barely any."

Grace realized she had a lot to learn about living at the ocean. "I think I need to get some books about Washington coastal living."

"Or just ask a local expert." He waggled his eyebrows. "Like myself. I'm available anytime, anywhere."

She laughed. "You're just trying to wriggle yourself further into my life."

"Is it working?"

When he turned his smile on like that, it was. They approached a spot on the beach where several cars were parked. Cade pulled in beside the last one and turned the engine off. "The wind can whip through a car with both doors open. Let me get out and come around to your side."

"All right."

Cade opened his door, glancing down the beach. "Well, shit," he mumbled under his breath.

"What's wrong?"

"Nothing." He shook his head. "Everything."

"Cade?"

"My parents are here."

Wow. The man did not sound excited about seeing his parents. "What's wrong with them being here?"

He turned in his seat to face her. "My parents and I don't see eye-to-eye. Haven't for a long time. My intention today was for us to have fun, get to know each other a little better. Not to drag you into my family drama."

At least he had both his parents. Grace shut the door on that thought quickly. "I've dealt with some pretty hard cases in the ER. Especially back in Chicago. I think I can deal with some strong-willed parents."

"You'd think that, but it's not always the case."

"The only way to find out is to meet them. And, against my better judgment, you got me out here to dig clams. You can't back out now. Besides, I think they've noticed your vehicle." She pointed out the window. Two people were headed their way.

"Then I'll just apologize now and hopefully, you'll understand."

That confused the hell out of Grace, but Cade had slammed his knit hat on his head and opened his door. The wind whistled into the car, making further talk impossible. Cade waved a hand to his parents as he hobbled around on one crutch and opened Grace's door. She'd pulled her own hat on and now, on the leeward side of the SUV, the wind died down and conversation was possible.

"Cade, dear, it's good to see you," his mother said, leaning in for the cheek kiss Cade offered. "What did you manage to injure now?"

"Nothing bad. Just an ankle sprain."

"It's those extreme sports of yours again, right?"

"Snowboarding isn't an extreme sport, Mother."

His mother backed a couple steps away and stared

at Grace with interest while his father shook Cade's gloved hand.

"Been a while, son."

"Yep."

"Who is this lovely creature with you?" his mother asked.

"Mother, Father, this is Grace Benson."

Grace noticed he didn't add doctor to her name. That didn't offend her, but something told her he'd left it off on purpose.

"Grace, this is Michelle and Lawrence, my parents."

"Dr. Michelle Huntington and Dr. Lawrence Huntington, if you please," his father said. "We've earned it."

Cade squeezed his eyes shut, proving what Grace had already suspected. He wanted to avoid all this doctor business. An unusual touch of the leprechaun snuck into Grace's soul and before she could squelch it, she held out her hand. "Dr. Benson, at your service."

Both Cade's parents' eyes widened. They kept looking between Grace and Cade, whereas Cade's eyes remained firmly shut as he shook his head.

His mother held tight to Grace's hand. "You're a doctor? Of medicine?"

"Yes, I work in the ER over at Grays Harbor General."

"Oh, it is so lovely to meet you. We own the clinic here in town."

The clinic she'd almost applied to for a job? Interesting. And if they owned the clinic, they had to be worth some money. Was that where Cade's expensive SUV had come from? Considering how red his face currently was, Grace couldn't imagine him taking money from his parents.

"I almost applied there, but chose instead to stay in the hospital setting."

"We'd have loved to have you. It's hard to find good doctors," his father said with a pointed stare at Cade.

"Maybe if you were more open-minded, you'd have the doctors you need."

"Maybe if you'd kept up with medical school, we wouldn't have to hire outsiders."

Ah, there was the wolf keeping good relationships at bay. They'd wanted their son to become a doctor and he'd chosen another direction. Cade was scowling so deeply now that Grace wasn't sure the day was redeemable, but she had to try. "Cade promised to teach me how to dig for clams," she said, hoping the change in subject would hold.

"We just bagged our limit." His father held up a mesh bag with what looked like rough rocks in it.

"Good, then you're done for the day," Cade said.

"We are. But you are welcome to join us for a clam dinner tonight."

"No, thank you."

The granite in his voice told Grace he didn't plan to give them the chance to find out more about her.

Once they'd walked off, Cade turned to her. "I'm really sorry about that."

"About what? Parents who are disappointed their son didn't become a doctor? If they can't get past your choices, they probably aren't worth the mental energy to think about. Now, about that clam digging?"

Cade reached inside the hoodie she'd pulled up, cupping her cheek. "You are amazing. I hope you know that." He leaned in, kissing her lightly on the lips, then moved back, too soon, to hold out his hand. He'd probably pay in pain later, trying to dig clams with one good leg and a crutch. Right now, that didn't matter one bit.

"Come on, let's get some dinner."

Chapter Five

They walked down near the water's edge where a few other people hunched over their shovels. The wind had fallen off some and Grace wanted to laugh at the squishy suction noise her rubber boots made as the wet sand tried to capture her. She felt like she was moving in two directions at once as the surf pulled sand from beneath her feet.

Cade, hopping on one foot, showed her how to look for the tiny holes in the wet sand, then how to go in fast and deep with the shovel, pulling a tube of muck out. And there, in the middle, was the ugliest looking clam she'd ever seen. Even so, when she found and dug up the first one all on her own, she whooped and hollered and danced around. The chilly weather and slight drizzle all disappeared in her joy that she'd captured this little piece of food in a shell.

"I got one!" she said to Cade, whose natural smile grew even wider as he watched her.

"Be careful. Clam digging can become an addiction," he said, laughing as he bagged her find.

"I believe you. Now come on, let's find some more."

For the next hour, they dug and laughed and dug until they limited out. Back at Cade's SUV, she tried to slip out of the boots, losing her balance and falling straight into Cade's arms. Because he was balanced on one leg, he slumped back against the vehicle as he caught her. She laughed, turning her face up to look at him. His smile disappeared and time slowed. His eyes darkened as he held her close.

"I really want to kiss you right now," he said, his voice husky.

Grace gulped, not sure she was ready for this. Staring up at him, everything in her thrummed with the desire to kiss him back. His gaze dipped to her lips and proved her undoing. Grace stopped thinking and reached for Cade, pulling his lips to hers with a sense of urgency that surprised her.

When their lips met, a shock of sensuality raced through her body, her heart thumping wildly. He persuaded her to open to him and his tongue explored the recesses of her mouth. Grace whimpered, awash in emotions. Confusion, need, raging desire. Time stood still as everything she felt coalesced into this moment when the only thing that mattered was him. And her. Together in the most basic sense. She clung to him, never wanting to let go. Sensation rolled through her over and over again as they learned each other's nuances.

When Cade lifted his head, Grace clutched him tighter, her hands bunching the fabric of his hoodie, wanting more, not ready for this to end.

With his breath as erratic as hers, Cade helped Grace into the SUV. As she settled into the seat, he lifted both his arms to lean on the frame, towering over her yet making her feel safer than she'd ever felt before.

"Wow." He drew in a deep breath.

"Yes." Grace reached up to smooth a finger along his lips. "These are pretty lethal."

Cade's thumb traced her own lips. "Not like these," he said. "I can't get my heart to slow down."

"I know the feeling." Grace shivered, though she couldn't tell if it was from the cold seeping in or the memory of Cade's lips on hers.

"You're getting cold. Come on, let's get these boots off and get warmed up."

"You mean warmed up again, right?"

His smile, just as lethal as his kisses, melted Grace to her very soul while he leaned down and pulled one boot off, then the other. His fingers lingered, tracing the curve of her ankle, and Grace almost curled her toes in delight. She flipped around in the seat and put her shoes on while he shut her door and opened the hatch. In the rearview mirror, she saw him toss the crutch in, take off his own boot and slip his shoe on. Soon, he was in the car, engine on and heat blasting to warm them up.

The chill had seeped right through Grace. She rubbed her cold hands together until Cade reached for them, cupping them in front of his face and blowing warm breath on them. Grace shivered, again not sure which stimulus her body was reacting to, the climbing ambient temperature or the heat emanating from the two of them.

"Ready for that hot cocoa?" Cade asked.

No. Grace wanted to make out some more. Desire must have flared in her eyes because he glanced down at her lips, then back up. "If I kiss you again, I won't want to stop."

Neither would Grace, but she needed to take this slowly. This attraction to Cade was a complication she hadn't planned for and she needed some time to think about it. So, taking a deep breath, she nodded. "Cocoa it is."

He flashed her a grin and put the SUV in drive, then recaptured her hand, settling it on his thigh as they drove down the beach.

Grace stared out the window at the waves crashing onto the shore, surprised to see how far the waterline had moved inward. Cade hadn't been kidding when he'd said the tidal movement covered a wide swath of beach. She looked forward to getting to know the rhythms of the Pacific Ocean as it gave and took away based on its own whim.

She also looked forward to getting to know Cade better. This attraction was such a surprise for her, and stronger than she'd felt with anyone else. That in itself scared her. But even fear couldn't mask how good it felt to have her hand in Cade's. How badly she wanted more of his kisses. More of everything.

Cade pulled into C&C Café and parked the Lexus, then, with a kiss to her knuckles, let her hand go and they both got out, Cade grabbing a crutch from the back seat.

"Connie makes the best cocoa in town," Cade said, guiding her toward the door with a hand to her back.

"You really should be using both crutches."

"But then I wouldn't have a hand free to touch you."

Grace shook her head, though her insides melted at his comment.

Inside, they shed their coats and looked around. The place was about half full, and more than one group had telltale boots on. Clammers abounded in here.

"Hey, Cade, how are you today?" A woman with salt and pepper hair wearing an apron rounded the counter.

"Doing well, Connie. Have you met Grace? She moved to Willow Bay a couple months ago."

"I don't think I have," Connie said, shaking Grace's hand and giving her a welcoming smile.

One of the best things about small-town life was how accepting everyone seemed to be. Grace smiled back. "It's nice to meet you."

"Grab a table anywhere and I'll be right over. With cocoa?"

"Definitely. Doubles," Cade answered.

"Yep, popular item on clamming days. Even got Gladys to sit down for a bit and enjoy one." Connie nodded toward the other side of the café where Gladys, cart beside her, watched them with interest. She waved, a big grin on her face. Cade waved back.

What was that about? Grace didn't have time to think it over. Cade indicated a booth and she slid in. He sat across from her.

"Less temptation," he said.

While Grace understood and agreed with him, a tiny part of her wished he'd chosen the dangerous road and sat next to her. Maybe a not-so-tiny part of her, either. Man, she was in big trouble. To distract herself, Grace looked around the café. She hadn't been lying to Cade when she said she ate mostly on the fly and mostly at the hospital or around there. This week was the first time she'd eaten out in Willow Bay and now here she was at her second restaurant in as many days.

"What's C&C stand for?" she asked.

"Connie, who you just met, and her husband, Charlie. He mostly works construction, but helps out here during the off-season."

The place had a fifties diner look to it, complete with small jukeboxes at each table. Grace twiddled the lever at the top and it shifted, showcasing the next page of songs to pick from. She looked up at Cade.

"They're real. Not plugged in, but real."

"The place is cute, or, as cute as it can be with the excessive holiday decorations." Excessive was an understatement. The café screamed Christmas, which made it feel cloying and claustrophobic to Grace, so she was glad when their cocoa came. Tall, steaming mugs with a heavenly scent. And, wouldn't you know it, a candy cane stuck in each one. She pulled hers out, set it on her napkin, and took a sip.

"Oh, this is wonderful," she said.

"I told you it would be. You've got a cocoa mustache." Cade reached over, braced his hand under her chin, and used his thumb to wipe the cocoa off. Grace decided then and there she needed more cocoa in her life.

Cade took a sip from his mug. "So, you don't like all the Christmas decorations here?"

A chill swept over Grace and she clutched her mug. This bordered on stuff she didn't talk about. "No, I don't."

He looked around, a wistfulness coming over him that Grace found endearing. "I love it. Christmas is all about going over the top."

Uh oh. Grace sent a quick plea out to the universe that Cade Huntington not be a Christmas junkie.

"Grace? You all right? You've gone white as a sheet."

"I—I'm fine." Damn, her voice was shaking. "Just not into all this."

"Not into the over-the-top kitsch or not into Christmas?"

"It's more about the holiday itself than it is the decorations."

Cade sat back in the booth, his fingers tapping his mug. "I don't know if I've ever met someone who didn't like Christmas."

Grace shrugged. She wasn't prepared to answer questions.

"Can I ask why?"

"No." Grace clutched her mug even harder, watching her hands turn white with the effort. The day had been so nice up until this. Christmas, as usual, ruined everything.

When Cade reached over and gently peeled her hands from around her mug, then looked at her with such patience and caring in his eyes, Grace found herself uncharacteristically near tears. She never cried.

"It's okay. We all have things we don't like, and if you and I were exactly the same, this relationship would be pretty boring. This is just something we'll need to work through at some point."

"I don't think so, Cade. I think this is where we stall." She wouldn't talk about this. Never had, even with her father. And never would. "I—I think I'd like to go home."

His frown deepening, Cade opened his mouth to argue. She could guess what he was going to say by the look on his face. Already, she knew him that well, and the hurt bit deep over what would not now happen. She'd known people who loved Christmas, had even dated a guy whose livelihood was designing and putting up holiday decorations at various businesses in Chicago. It didn't work out. It couldn't when the holiday was nothing but a bitter pill for her to swallow every year.

Somehow, Cade chose not to press the issue. Grace was thankful. He stood, pulled his wallet out, and dropped some bills on the table. He reached for her coat and helped her into it, then let her lead out to the car. They drove back to her place without saying a word. When he put the SUV in park outside her house and turned to her, Grace opened the door, knowing she needed to get out of there before she cried the tears she'd refused to shed for years. She mentally set her backbone to rigid. She could do this.

"Grace, I don't understand your reaction. It's just a holiday."

"My aversion to Christmas is not something I will ever discuss. I can tell you love this holiday, but I don't. I won't. Ever. Good night, Cade. Thank you for a wonderful day."

At least, it had been wonderful. Right up to this moment. Grace leaped out of the car before he could say anything else and fled up her steps. She fumbled with her house key, finally managing to get the door open. Grateful that Cade hadn't tried to join her, she slipped inside and closed the door.

Finally, the tears fell. Tears for a life not lived, for a mother who hadn't cared. A mother whose actions had left Grace so personally screwed up that when something good finally came along, she tossed it in the garbage along with the holiday she hated.

Grace slumped to the floor, more miserable than she'd been since that fateful Christmas. She clutched her head, not wanting to think about it, feel it. Not again. Never again. Still in her coat, she hung her head and let the tears fall. Minutes later, she heard Cade's SUV pull away.

She couldn't help but think that the best thing that had ever happened to her had just driven out of her life.

~~~

Cade drove across town to his place deep in thought and confused as hell. What had just happened? The day had started out awesome. He'd convinced her to come clamming with him, which had been in serious doubt when he'd shown up at her door. Granted, running into the folks had put a damper on things, at least for him, but she'd kind of defended him with them. He'd liked that.

The whole thing with Christmas, though. Wow, what a nosedive. It was obvious to him that her feelings went beyond a mere dislike of Christmas. She had a deep-seated aversion to the holiday. Or maybe it was fear? He couldn't tell, but her walls had slammed firmly into place and she wasn't letting anyone in. Including him.

He'd never met anyone who didn't like Christmas, so it was difficult to fathom what could have made her hate the holiday so much. They'd barely started to get to know each other. He didn't even know if her parents were alive or if she had siblings.

But he was damn sure going to find out. He'd kissed a lot of women in his life, but never had he felt like he did when kissing Grace. It wasn't so much the kissing that had rocked his world. Something had clicked into place while he held her. She had settled it. Somehow, he gained something that he hadn't even known was missing from his life.

And he wasn't about to let that go.

Cade parked in his garage, shut off his alarm system, and went inside. He put the clams in the fridge. There were too many for him and he'd hoped to share them with Grace. He'd make a burger and salad for dinner. Maybe tomorrow, he'd figure out a way to coax her over to his house so he could cook for her.

Just how he would accomplish that, he had no idea. His cell rang and he glanced at it, rolling his eyes. Knowing his mother would call every half hour until he answered, he hit the green button.

"Hi, Mom."

"Hello. I'm not interrupting anything, am I?" The hope in her voice caused eyeroll number two.

"Not at all. What's up?"

"Oh, I just wanted to say we had a lovely time today, and it was so nice to meet your Dr. Benson. She seems absolutely enchanting."

Enchanting. That was a good word for Grace. She'd enchanted him. "Thanks, Mom. If that's all?"

"Is she there? I thought maybe we could meet up for coffee one of these days, talk about the clinic. And her work, of course."

There it was. She wanted to pitch the clinic to Grace.

Not going to happen. Ever, if Cade had any choice in the matter, which, when it came to his parents, he rarely did. The only way Cade got his way was to walk in the opposite direction.

"Grace just started her job. You can't headhunt her for your clinic."

"I never said I wanted to do that."

"It was inferred."

"We're short-staffed, Cade. If you'd gone to medical school like you should have, we wouldn't be in this situation. But your father and I aren't getting any younger and we'll never be able to retire if we don't find some coverage."

"Then sell the place." He'd love to be done with the clinic. It had become the bane of his existence. His parents never understood his need to do something else, something all his own.

"We can't sell the clinic. That's our legacy. It was supposed to be yours, too."

"It isn't the legacy I want."

"So you've said. It's not too late, Cade. You're still young enough to go back to school and get your medical degree. Your new friend would probably love having a doctor as a partner."

"Wow, you've already got us married off, don't you, Mom? Look, I hate to be blunt, but I know that's really all that gets through to you. This thing with Grace is new. Don't butt in. I will never become the doctor you want. Ever. I'm happy with what I do. Now, I love you and Dad, but I need to go. Goodbye."

His mother would go to her grave still arguing, so Cade hit the red button, disconnecting the call. He opened the fridge and got out fixings to make a veggie burger and a salad, setting them on the kitchen island. Gripping the edges of the counter, Cade stared at the food, all desire to eat gone. His mother frustrated him, and the situation with Grace frustrated him. He was so keyed up, he couldn't eat if he wanted to. Instead, he headed downstairs to his basement and the gym equipment he kept there.

Being limited to upper body workouts wasn't a problem. An hour later, he was sweaty, worn out, and not one bit closer to knowing how he was going to ease either situation. All he knew was that he wouldn't let Grace go easily. He had to at least try to bring her back. No longer hungry, Cade put the food back in the fridge and headed for his shower, determined to find a way.

Chapter Six

Once again, Cade sat outside Grace's house without an invitation and without giving her any prior knowledge of his arrival. After a night of tossing and turning, he'd decided the only thing to do was to rip off the Band-Aid. She was a physician. She'd understand that. At least, he hoped she would. He'd pulled together some things and now, in the damp, misty midafternoon, here he sat. Determined to not let go without a fight, he got out, draped greenery around his neck, grabbed a bag of supplies, and marched toward her front steps.

"I wouldn't do that, young man."

Cade stopped and turned to see Gladys rambling down the sidewalk toward him.

"A bit further out than your normal roaming, aren't you, Gladys?"

"Gotta keep an eye on things. Besides, it's good for these old bones to walk. Keeps that bone-density stuff strong."

He chuckled, then the soft pings of a windchime caused him to look at Grace's house. It was small, but her front porch had been built for summers when people sat outside in rocking chairs and visited with the neighbors. He'd envisioned what it would look like with a light touch of holiday spirit and had picked up cedar garland and ribbons for just that purpose. Not outright Christmas decorations, but more of a winter spirit. That's what he was doing for her. At least, that's what he'd convinced himself he was doing.

"Don't do it."

"Don't do what?"

"I saw the look on that girl's face at Connie's yesterday. For some reason, she's got a powerful dislike of the holidays. Until you figure that out, this isn't gonna have the effect you want it to."

Cade almost asked how she knew his plans, but he'd been caught dead to rights with garland around his neck. "How do you even know she lives here?"

"I know everything in this town," Gladys said, rambling past him. "Don't you forget that. And mind what I said. She's not going to react well to this. Nosiree. Not at all." She chuckled as she walked on down the street pushing her rickety Mabel.

First, Cade stared at the house, then at the departing Gladys, then back at the house. Deciding, he bounded up the steps to Grace's porch. *Rip off that bandaid.* The thought kept him focused, even while he skated on thin ice. This was for her, for them. Cade crossed his fingers and went to work. He'd finished putting the garland up and was halfway through placing the red ribbons when her front door whipped open. Distracted by the tight yoga pants and workout shirt she had on, Cade didn't see the fire in her eyes until she got right up next to him.

"What the hell do you think you're doing?" she said, her voice eerily low.

Uh oh. She was pissed. Beyond pissed, if Cade was any good at reading people. "It's just a garland and some ribbons. Seasonal decorations," he said, hearing the lameness in his words.

She put both hands on her hips, distracting him again. "I told you, I don't do Christmas."

"They're not—"

"Take them down."

Cade worried he wasn't going to be able to turn this around. "Wait. Please. I'm not trying to make you angry. I'm trying to help."

Grace, apparently, was done talking. She marched over to the railing, ripped off the two red ribbons he'd affixed, then started tearing at the greenery, destroying it. "Stop, please," Cade begged. "All right, all right. I'll take it down." He put his hands over hers and she yanked them away. With a glare, she turned, marched back into her house, and slammed the door.

As he took down the greenery and put it back in his truck, Cade realized he'd made a horrible mistake, forcing the issue. If a person didn't like Christmas, that was one thing. If a person was afraid of Christmas, that was quite another. And he understood now what Gladys had tried to tell him. Grace feared this holiday, a fear that was far from healthy. Anger welled up in him. Something terrible must have happened to Grace in the past to cause this strong reaction. And he damn well wanted to figure out what it was. He wanted to help her through it.

Driving through town, he tried to make sense of her reaction. She'd built her walls so high and tight around her that he wanted to cheer every time he saw a chink in them. But this? This was a huge barrier, and well-defended. He had no idea how to get past it.

His stomach rumbled, so he pulled into Square Peg Pizza for an early dinner.

"Hi, Cade," Paul said from behind the counter.

"You covering the restaurant?" Cade asked, sitting on a counter stool. Having grown up in Willow Bay, Cade knew Bernie, who'd run away from a troubled home when she was just a kid, had worked hard to buy the restaurant from the retiring owner. The business was thriving. Paul, her husband, worked with at-risk youth and was lucky to be able to stagger his hours as needed.

"Bernie wasn't feeling very well so she's resting." He pointed upstairs to their seaside-cute apartment. Cade had put cable in for Bernie.

"Pregnancy stuff?"

Paul nodded, whisking a hand through his perennially disheveled hair.

"I wouldn't worry too much," Cade said. "Women have a way of getting through it all. I swear, they are stronger than we are."

Paul chuckled, then sobered. "Doesn't make me worry any less."

"I get that." Cade looked around the empty restaurant. "Not too busy, eh?"

"The dinner rush hasn't started yet. Can I get you something?"

"Yeah, a veggie pizza to go."

"Ahhh, Bernie's special pizza, then."

"Yes. And, I think I need to drown my sorrows. How about an O'Doul's."

Paul laughed. "You can drown your sorrow in non-alcoholic beer?"

"Better than water, at least at the moment."

"Okay, one O'Doul's coming up." Paul popped the cap, set the bottle in front of Cade, then went in back to make the pizza.

Cade looked around at the restaurant's eclectic décor. Old license plates, movie posters, farm implements, and one great, big carved wooden bear holding a large, bright orange peanut. With an equally bright orange knit cap set jauntily over one ear. Cade smiled at the variety, a crazy collection of stuff that made Square Peg a fun place to eat. He'd like to bring Grace here. Except, Christmas lights and greenery adorned every corner and wall. She wouldn't see the place the way he did while all the extra decorations were up. Maybe after the holidays.

If there was an after. Cade took a swig of his beer and twirled the bottle on the counter. He stared as it turned, trying to figure out how to fix the mess he'd created.

"Looks like some dark thoughts going on in that head of yours." Paul pulled up a stool on his side of the counter and sat. "Want to talk about it?"

Cade took another pull off his beer. "Not sure I should."

"I get that."

"Maybe I just need to back off."

Paul got up and poured himself a glass of water, then sat back down. "Back off what?"

"I'm seeing someone."

"You're always seeing someone." Paul chuckled. "Different someones."

"This one's really different. Important. And skittish."

"Oh, so the chase is on, huh?"

Cade shook his head. "It's not like that. She's not like anyone I've ever met. I don't want to chase her. I just want to be with her. Except, this is apparently the worst time of year to do that. She's not into the holidays."

Paul's eyes widened. "Umm, has she seen your house?"

"Not yet. And after this afternoon, I'm dreading that, if I even get the chance to show her."

"You always think you know the best thing for people, Cade. And then you go off half-cocked on those ideas. What did you do?"

Taking another pull of his beer, Cade figured he should just admit how stupid he'd been. "I surprised her by putting up Christmas decorations on her front porch."

"Oh, no." Paul shook his head.

"Yeah. She went ballistic on me. Now that I've put a little distance between me and my stunt, I see she might be right. I just... Paul, I think she's actually afraid of Christmas. I have no idea why, but I want to help her past that. I'd love for her to find the joy of the season."

Paul leaned his elbows on the counter. "I work with a lot of frightened kids."

Cade nodded.

"And most of them put up a front of bravado. They think the fear doesn't show, that they can manage it if they keep up that tough exterior."

"That's actually a lot like her."

"You know that old saying about bringing a horse to water?"

Shit. Cade didn't like the idea of waiting for Grace to come around in her own time. That wasn't his style. He fixed things.

"I don't even know why she's afraid."

"The only way to get that story is to be patient and give her space. Maybe wait until after the holidays?" Paul looked up at the ceiling. "Believe me, with women especially, it can take a lot of patience. But it's worth it in the end."

A timer dinged. Paul pulled Cade's pizza from the oven and boxed it up. Cade finished his beer, paid his tab, and picked up the box.

Paul glanced at Cade's ankle boot. "Looks like you should be keeping weight off that thing."

"Crutches are in the car. Figured this quick a trip wouldn't hurt too bad." Cade put weight on the ankle and winced. "Might have been wrong about that. Hey, thanks." Cade shook Paul's hand. "I appreciate the advice. I know I need to wait this out. I'll try, but I'm kind of like a bull in a china shop. That's not easy to change."

"It's not. But it will be worth it."

"Yeah. Lots to think about."

Which Cade did, all the way home and while he sat at his kitchen island eating pizza. With no easy solution in sight, he was edgy and full of frustration, so he headed down to the basement to his workout gear. He hoped that, even without using the ankle, he could tire himself out enough for a quick nap, then work into the evening. He hadn't gotten much sleep last night. What he really wanted to do was rush over to Grace's house and beg her forgiveness. Paul was right, though. He needed to give her time. Patience really wasn't his strong suit, but he'd try.

With all the frustration workouts he was doing, if nothing else, he'd be well-toned.

~~~

Cade finished his workout and lay on the couch just in time for his phone to ring. Bleary-eyed, he answered it without looking, hoping it was Grace.

It wasn't.

"Hi, Mom." He lay on his back, his ankle throbbing even after ice, and ran a hand through his hair.

"Good evening. I hope I haven't interrupted anything."

The hope in her voice made him cringe.

"What can I help you with? We just spoke yesterday."

"I know, but I don't think I was clear enough. We were delighted to meet Dr. Benson."

Always use the title. That was his mother's mantra.

"We'd like to invite you both over to dinner. You pick the night and we'll make it work."

Right now, he'd be happy if Grace would just talk to him. Even that might be a thing of the past. And parental interference, especially from *his* parents, would only make matters worse. Cade decided to try some honesty, though his mother would ram on forward no matter what he said. Experience had taught him that.

"Mom, Grace and I are just getting to know each other. Neither of us knows if this will go any further and I'm not going to bring her to dinner until we've had more time together."

"You are such a slowpoke. Look at your father and me."

Cade knew the story well. They'd met in residency, married a month later, and were very close to having forty-five years of married bliss checked off on that master to-do list of theirs.

"Not everyone knows as quickly as you did."

"She's a catch, Cade. Both your father and I see that. Don't let her get away."

Because you want my happiness or because you want another doctor for your precious clinic? Tempted to ask the question, Cade clamped his mouth shut.

"I can't talk right now. I'm working," he finally said.

"Give some thought to dinner and let us know."

"I will. Love you." Cade punched the button to end the call. He rolled to set the phone on the coffee table next to him, causing a stab of pain in his ankle. It took a long time for that pain to subside, and even longer for his brain to shut off the what-if conversation he kept having with himself.

Chapter Seven

Grace limped across the dark parking lot to her car after a very strange ending to her twelve-hour day shift in the ER. An angry man had tried to yank his battered wife out of the ER before the police could get there. Grace got in his way and he'd stomped on her foot. Hard. And now here she was, hobbling around on a bruised-but-not-broken foot. The quick diagnosis was a bonus for choosing ER work. Fast, free X-rays. Thankfully, a lot of the cases she'd seen today had been fine. Or better, like the woman with abdominal pain that turned out to be a viable pregnancy after years of infertility. Grace had smiled as the prospective parents walked out arm in arm, in happy shock, headed home to months of bed rest that they didn't mind one bit. She'd treated a kid who'd fallen and cut open his eyebrow, needing stitches, and successfully stabilized two heart attacks. She'd quickly handed one appendectomy off to the surgical unit, fearing a rupture was in progress. A pretty full day, but not full enough to keep her thoughts totally on work.

She kept replaying yesterday's fight with Cade. After she'd come unglued on him, she'd raced inside and slammed the door, mostly to keep him from seeing her in full-on panic mode. She'd leaned against that door, shaking, breathing shallow, unable to focus on any one thing. When she finally calmed down enough to move to the couch, an hour had passed. And Luna had stuck very close to her side.

Her stomach filled with churning acid, she'd gotten a glass of water and sank back onto the couch. She didn't do Christmas. What about that statement made Cade think he could change her mind with a few decorations? And his lack of respect, doing that without asking? She never wanted to see him again.

Except she did. That was the problem. Cade was there, in her mind and heart, all day long. She'd picked up her cell phone to call him several times since their fight, setting it back down each time without making the call. Even now, she itched to punch his number and talk while she drove home. Grace had never needed someone to pull her out of her work day and help her relax. She'd shouldered that burden herself and had done very well, though sometimes it wasn't easy. What was it like, having a partner to help you see the good side of life? Her father hadn't had that since she'd been eight years old. He'd turned into a lonely man. Yet he'd never become bitter. Her father had done everything he could to make her childhood a good one, and he'd never remarried. Her mother had done a number on him, too.

Grace didn't want to grow old alone. But damn it, some lines deserved respect and Cade had crossed a big one. She didn't talk about why Christmas bothered her, not to anyone. Did he really think he could coax it out of her with garland?

It had been a while since she'd called her father and it wasn't too late for him back east, so Grace tapped the hands-free button and rang his number. Her father's enthusiasm over her call had made her both happy and guilt-riddled. She really did need to call him more.

"How you doing with the season, kiddo?" he asked.

"Okay, Dad."

"You don't sound okay."

"Some things are... making this season extra difficult."

"Things? Or someone?"

"Why would you go directly there?"

"Because you've gotten pretty good at ignoring the holidays so there must be a someone tugging at you. Want to talk about it?"

"Not really." Her dad had never been one to talk about heart stuff, and they hadn't discussed Christmas much since that night, so it surprised her that he would try to get her to talk about it now.

"Is he a good man?"

"Seems to be." That wasn't the truth. Grace knew Cade was a good man. His love for Christmas confronted by her absolute hatred of it was a big barrier between them, though.

Her father sighed. "I'm not big on giving advice, Gracie. But I think it's time to let the past go. It's eating you up, devouring any chance at happiness, just like it did to me."

Grace's foot came off the gas pedal, she was so shocked by his statement. Like her, her father had held onto the pain all these years. What had changed? "Have you put the past behind you, Dad?"

"Not completely, no. I'll admit I still have some trust issues."

"That's why you haven't found anyone to share your life with, isn't it?"

She could almost hear him nodding, except his next statement sent that picture straight out of her head.

"Actually, I might have."

"Might have what?"

"Found someone."

In shock for the second time, Grace pulled the car over and put it in park. Her father had been single since Grace's eighth Christmas. "You're seeing someone?"

"Have been for a while. Her name is Jackie. She owns a restaurant I frequent and we just got to talking. She's really nice and, well, she's being patient with me and my issues."

Jackie. Grace didn't know any Jackies. Funny thing to think about when your father just told you he's dating for the first time in twenty years. Grace wasn't sure how she felt about it.

"I'm happy, Gracie. I'm finally letting go of the pain. I held onto it for way too long. You have, too. Maybe you should give Christmas, and this guy, a chance. What's the worst that could happen?"

She could be abandoned again. Her heart broken again. She could have to start all over again. "I— I don't know, Dad."

"Just think about it. And I'd really like you to meet Jackie one of these days. Maybe, after the holidays are over, we can come out for a visit, see where you work, and you two could get to know each other."

"I'd like that a lot."

Grace rang off the call and pulled back onto the road, still reeling from the news that her father had a girlfriend and that he'd put the past mostly behind him. This was the one thing they'd always had in common, holding onto their anger and sense of betrayal. If he'd put it behind him, she was now alone in her pain. And weary, hanging on to the negative emotions. Was it time to let them out, let them go?

When Grace turned onto the main street of Willow Bay, she spied the now-familiar shopping cart being pushed by the bundled-up Gladys. Grace pulled over and rolled down her window.

"How are you feeling, Gladys?"

"Oh, I'm doing just fine, dearie. How are you?" Gladys put a hand on the car and speared Grace with a look that seemed to drive straight into her soul. What was it with this woman?

"I'm fine. So no aftereffects from the other night?" Guilt at almost hitting the homeless woman still sat in her craw like a spike.

"Oh, no." Gladys waved the thought away. "Just let that go. I'm fine. You, on the other hand— " Gladys leaned in. "You look like you're not sleeping well."

How could the woman tell that in the dim overhead light from her car? "Just tired from a long day at work."

Gladys's look said she wasn't buying Grace's story.

"You know, I saw you a couple days ago at the diner with that nice Cade Huntington."

Grace stiffened. This was getting way too personal and it was way past time to get on with her night. "Do you need a ride anywhere? I'm happy to drop you."

The old woman shook her head. "I'm fine. Just wanted to say Cade's good people. You could do a lot worse. Have you seen his house? He takes Christmas to a whole new level. Good for the spirit, that boy is."

A whole new level? Nope. Not something Grace wanted to experience in any way, but Gladys, the town meddler, didn't need to know that. "Well, then, I'll let you get on to, uh, wherever you're headed."

With a final wave, Gladys backed up, grabbed Mabel's handle, and ambled off down the street. Grace watched her for a minute, then pulled out, thinking about Cade. It made sense that his house was overloaded with holiday cheer. Grace shook her head. Attracted to a guy who loves Christmas. Could this be any more complicated?

Without realizing it, Grace drove right past her street, straight through a Willow Bay overlit with holiday cheer. She drove to the far side, to Cade's house, an address her damn memory retained from his hospital visit. Something deep inside had tugged her in that direction. Plus, through all the thinking, the memories, and the shoring up of her walls the last couple days, one thought kept wandering through her brain. Just how bad was his house? Grace was almost afraid to find out.

Once she'd turned onto his street, she discovered Cade wasn't the only holiday lover on the block. The entire street was lit up. The centerpiece, a house with modern touches like black-bordered windows, seemed to be the showpiece. Number 686. Cade's.

To say the house had Christmas lights seriously understated things. Cade had strung lights on every horizontal and vertical line of the house. Santa and his sleigh and reindeer brightly lit the roof. Wow. The blanket web lights over every shrub, and the strings wrapped on the branches and trunk of his one mature tree, added up to nothing short of a spectacle. Plus, there were one, two, three, *four* huge blow-up decorations.

Wow. Wow. Wow. The man really did go all out for Christmas. Seeing this depressed Grace. How could they test the waters between them if he over-indulged in the holidays and she abhorred them?

Tap. Tap.

Grace nearly leaped out of her seatbelt as someone tapped on her window. She turned her head to find Cade standing there. Damn. Caught in the act of spying. She lowered the window. At least he was using his crutches.

"I saw your car," he said, his voice subdued. "Thought I'd come see if you needed anything."

"I—I— "

"You wanted to see if I was as into Christmas as I said?"

"Yes." No sense denying it.

Cade smiled. "I'm glad you came. Want to come

in?"

Unsure if she wanted to see if the inside of Cade's house was as over the top as the outside, Grace hedged. "Oh, no, I couldn't. I just got off duty. I'm still in scrubs."

"No pressure, but if you haven't eaten, I was just about to sit down to dinner and there's enough for two."

Her stomach grumbled at that moment, and they both chuckled.

"Come on. It's just dinner."

Nothing was "just" anything with Cade. The man went larger than life on everything, including dating. "I should still be angry with you."

"I can't deny that. I earned it, and I'm sorrier than I can say. So, dinner?"

Grace stared at the house again. "Is it as decorated inside as it is outside?"

"Pretty much."

With a roll of her eyes, she weighed her options. When her stomach growled again, she gave in to the offending organ and nodded, though hesitantly. Could she handle all this Christmas?

Cade smiled and reached for her car door as she shut off the engine. Grace stepped out, forgetting about her bum foot.

"Ouch!"

Before she fell flat on her face, Cade steadied her. "What happened to your foot?"

"ER patient. It's a long story that I probably can't tell because of HIPAA guidelines."

"Well, come on then. Let's gimp together up the steps and into the house. Need one of my crutches?" He held one out with enough hope showing on his face to lighten Grace's mood.

"I think I can manage without a crutch, but thank you."

"You sure? I thought I could, too. Turns out, I was way wrong. I should have listened to my doctor."

"Yes, you should have." She eased the sting with a bit of a smile and together they limped inside, where Grace stopped short, panic welling up inside her. "You weren't kidding."

"'Tis the season," Cade said, helping her out of her coat.

His two-story house had a black metal banister that contrasted with the plethora of garland, ribbon, and lights wound around it. All the way up the stairs. Every picture she could see on the wall had been covered with festive wrap and ribbons. The runner on the floor of the hallway was green and red.

At the back, the open concept and tall ceilings were dwarfed by the biggest tree she'd ever seen indoors, except maybe at a mall. "How did you get the star on top?"

"Ten-foot ladder and a reach," he said. "Come, sit down and rest that foot. Want something to drink?"

Grace stared at the tree. Every year, her father had put one up and tried to help her move on. Every year, she'd refused to have anything to do with it. Maybe this will be a good test for her. She'll just have to keep her eyes on Cade to distract her. He was a pretty good distraction, after all.

"Just water," Grace said, moving a blanket emblazoned with Santa Clause and sitting on the couch. She put her foot up on the ottoman in front of her and sighed with relief.

"I have ibuprofen, too, if you'd like some."

"I took some before I left. I mostly just need to stay off this foot for a while."

"Relax, then." Cade hobbled over on one crutch and set a bottle of chilled water beside her. "Want a glass?"

"No. This is fine. Thank you."

"Great. Rest. I've got a couple things to do in the kitchen, then I'll bring dinner out."

"Oh, I can help." She started to get up.

Cade rested a hand on her shoulder. "Please, Grace. Just relax. Let me do this for you."

The sincere wish to help that softened his eyes almost made her tear up. She'd been so mean to him. And no one had ever given her this much consideration or tried to see beyond the Ice Queen. Grace nodded, staring down at her hands, afraid if she looked up at him again, she'd start blubbering. She hadn't blubbered in twenty years.

So tired. She rested her head back on the pillow. The past few days had taken a lot out of her. She closed her eyes and tried to sort through her feelings.

When she opened them, she found herself slumped deep into the couch cushions and disoriented. Where was she?

"Good morning, sleepyhead," Cade said, smiling at her.

"Good God, is it morning?" Had she been asleep on his couch all night? And had he been watching her all this time? Grace smoothed back hair that had escaped from her work bun.

"Don't worry. You've only been asleep for about half an hour. And I didn't see your mouth wide open or one bit of drool. In fact, you look as lovely in sleep as you do awake."

Another first, his compliment.

"I'm so sorry."

"Don't be. You've had a long day and needed some rest. And dinner kept quite well. If you feel alert enough, I'll bring it over so we can eat."

"You waited for me?"

"Of course."

One of her internal walls fell with a jarring thunk as

a little bit of joy slipped into Grace's soul. She could shore it back up, but she just didn't want to. "May I use the bathroom?"

"Sure." Cade reached out a hand to help her stand. She stood there, staring at their entwined hands. His felt warm, comforting. Like home.

"Past the kitchen, door on the left."

Grace hobbled through the kitchen where something smelled really delicious, causing her stomach to growl. A few minutes later, much more composed after seeing herself in the mirror, she joined Cade at the couch. He'd pushed the ottoman to the side and pulled the low coffee table in. Two plates of food sat waiting.

"I hope you don't mind. I dished you up."

"I don't mind at all." Grace settled herself on the couch and Cade handed her utensils, napkin, and, finally her plate. "This smells really good," she said.

"Tastes good too, a crab risotto recipe I've refined to my liking. The salad is lettuce, cranberries, feta, and walnuts drizzled with a vinegar and honey mustard dressing. Oh, you're not allergic to nuts, are you?"

"No allergies, thankfully." Grace took a bite of salad. "This is heavenly."

Cade reached for a bowl still on the coffee table. "Bread? It's a sourdough loaf I get from the bakery in town. That place is Willow Bay's best-kept secret."

"Thank you." Grace took a piece.

"Do you need butter?"

"No. From the smell of it, this bread can stand on its own."

He beamed at her. "Right answer."

Everything was perfect, or would be if it weren't for that damn tree. *Don't look at the tree, Grace, hard as it is to miss. Concentrate on the risotto, the delicious, crabby risotto.*

They each settled back on the couch, propped up their gimped feet, and enjoyed their meal in silence. Or relative silence. Grace couldn't help uttering a few mmmms and yums. "This all tastes great. Where did you learn to cook like this?"

"My mother made sure we knew how to cook. Being single, for a while there I was eating out a lot. I kept thinking of ways I'd change the different things I tried to better match my palate. Finally, I just gave up eating out. Now, I make most of my meals from scratch. Except sometimes, when I'm lucky enough to meet nice doctors in restaurants." He smiled.

"Well, you are a very good cook," Grace said to hide her reaction to his compliment. She wasn't used to this.

"Thank you. I enjoy it. Do you cook?"

Grace shook her head. "At least, I don't cook much. I like a good, healthy breakfast so I'll make myself an egg white omelet some days. Mostly, I eat at the hospital or grab something on my way home."

"That's a shame. You're missing out on a lot of great taste sensations. I'll have to cook you a proper meal one of these nights."

This meal was heaven and he didn't consider it proper? She'd have to compare it to what he thought was a good meal. And, right now, Grace wanted the chance to make that comparison. She wanted to have more dinners with Cade, to get to know him better.

Glancing around at all the holiday décor, a combination of crafty, beautiful, and kitschy, she wondered how to get past it all.

Cade took her plate and set it on the coffee table. The movement, when he settled back on the couch, brought him closer to her. Close enough that he stretched his arm out and began to lightly massage her neck, an amazing feeling and another first for Grace.

"I'm truly sorry I didn't respect your wishes, that I tried to decorate your house, Grace. I didn't realize the depth of your feelings about Christmas. Or I chose not to realize. Either way, it wasn't right and I can't apologize enough."

His apology was sincere. His tone proved that. And his hands felt so good, so relaxing. Grace wanted to give herself over to his ministrations, to lean in and forget everything but Cade's hand rubbing her neck. To kiss him with wanton abandon and be kissed by him.

Maybe you should give Christmas, and this guy, a chance. Her father's words came back to her. Grace didn't know if she was ready for this, but she wanted time with Cade like she'd never wanted anything before. But first, he deserved some answers. Grace straightened and turned toward him, wrapping one leg beneath her and moving out of range of his healing hand. Not far enough, though, as he settled said hand on her knee.

"I need to tell you why I don't like Christmas."

"You don't have to tell me anything. It's all right."

"I want to tell you. I've held this close to my chest for a lot of years."

Cade nodded, full of attentiveness.

"I, um, I'm close to my dad. It's been just the two of us for a long time, but when I spoke to him tonight, he told me he's seeing someone."

"That's good, right?" Cade asked, rubbing a thumb along the inner bend in her knee, distracting her.

Grace nodded. "It took me a minute to get used to the idea. He hasn't dated, or wanted to date, for twenty years. Ever since my mother walked out on us."

She paused, working up the ability to finish the story.

"Your mother left you at Christmas, didn't she?" Cade asked quietly.

With another nod, Grace swallowed the bile in her throat and tried to continue. How could this feel so raw after so much time? "I was eight. It was late Christmas Eve and I'd been sent to bed a couple hours earlier. Like any kid, I snuck downstairs to see if I could catch Santa in the act. Before I got there, I saw Mom come through from the back of the house with a suitcase. She put her coat on and checked herself in the mirror. She must have seen me out of the corner of her eye because she turned and looked right at me. She told me I was supposed to be in bed. I asked her where she was going.

"'Just going to the store to get a few last-minute things,' she said. She looked surprised when I asked her about the suitcase.

"She glanced at the case behind her, then back at me. I remember so clearly what she said. 'The better to disguise what I'm bringing home, angel.'

"Somehow, I knew her words didn't ring true. She kissed me on the cheek, but it felt hollow."

Grace stared at the Christmas tree. "I spent all that night in front of our tree, waiting for her to come home. I fell asleep at some point and woke up to see my dad standing there, tears in his eyes, holding a letter in his hand.

"She's gone, Gracie."

Reaching for a pom-pom snowman on the end table, Grace smoothed the red plaid muffler around its neck. "He said it had nothing to do with me, but that was all. A few days later, I snuck into his room and found the letter. It took me a bit to read it and I didn't understand all of it at the time, but the gist of it was that she didn't want to live in poverty anymore. She'd found someone who offered her a better life, a more lavish life.

"The thing is, my Dad's a carpenter and he makes decent money. Enough that he helped me get through college and med school without too much debt." Grace shook her head. "I don't know what she needed beyond that, but we never saw or heard from her again."

Embarrassed by her tears, Grace swiped at her cheeks. Cade reached out and pulled her into his arms.

They sat there, staring at the brightly lit tree, taking silent time. For Grace, to finally tell someone the story was cathartic. For Cade, well, he had to be digesting it.

"You don't have any idea where she is?"

Against Cade's chest, Grace shook her head. "Never heard from her again. Dad waited five years, then filed for an uncontested divorce."

"Have you ever thought of hiring someone to find her?"

"Why? Everything I know about my mother paints her as shallow and unloving. She never cared about us. Knowing where she is wouldn't change anything, so no, I don't care to ever find her. My dad worked really hard to give me a good life and make up for the love I missed from a mother who only cared about herself. I'm content with that. Well, except for Christmas. And I don't tolerate lies. Not big on people thinking they are better than me because they have money, either." Grace swiped at her face and sat up. "In fact, I don't care if I ever make more money than I do right now. That's why I didn't consider working for your parents and went to work at a small community hospital. I have a modest income that I can comfortably live on and that's all I need. That's really all I want."

~ ~ ~

So many emotions raced through Cade, it took everything he had to keep it in. He wanted to rage for that little girl, abandoned by her mother. To race out and find her and show her what she missed. He wanted to hug her father for doing everything in his power to give Grace a normal childhood. He wanted to pound something.

He watched Grace look around the comfortable room. He could see her mind working. Dread filled his stomach.

"This is pretty nice living for a cable installer," she

said.

He steeled himself against his emotions while he tried to figure out what to say. She hated liars and she was none too fond of rich people. He needed to convince her to give him a chance. If he told her he'd made millions from digital game design, he'd lose his chance.

Gulping down his guilt, he offered the half-truth. "The company pays me pretty well since they have trouble finding someone in this area."

"This place doesn't look cheap."

"I'm really good at finding deals, but yeah, I do okay. I'm really sorry, Grace, that you had to go through all that as a child. It makes me angry for you."

Grace let out a long sigh. "I've never told anyone that story. Ever. I guess maybe my dad's girlfriend knows now. And you. You're the only ones who know."

"I can understand your aversion to Christmas. Walking out on Christmas Eve? Wow. What was she thinking?"

"I'll never know."

Cade stood and pulled Grace up and into his arms. "I'm really glad you told me."

She leaned against him, her head tucked under his chin. The protective instinct flared inside Cade. Nothing else mattered but keeping Grace safe. And happy.

"I need to find a way to let this go," she said.

"This seems like a good start," Cade answered.

"I still don't want any decorations on my house." Grace moved her head back to look at him.

Hands out to his side, Cade swore he'd never do that again without permission. Her hazel eyes were bright with lingering tears and Cade saw an openness within them that sent him spiraling into a place he'd never been before. Emotion overwhelmed him. He cupped her cheeks like they were fragile china and leaned in.

"I'd like to kiss you, Grace. Would you allow me to do that?"

"Yes," she whispered, her breath brushing him like a warm summer breeze. His lips moved across hers, feather-light. He kissed the corners of her mouth where her lips quirked up when she smiled. Unable to settle the feelings whirling through him, he captured her mouth, devouring her and being equally devoured.

Kissing, hugging, feeling, they swayed back and forth—cohesive, fluid, and wanting the same thing. God, he wanted her like nothing else.

"Ow."

Cade pulled back. "What's wrong? Did I hurt you?" He'd lost himself in her. Had he done something to cause her pain?

"No. I kind of forgot myself and put too much weight on my foot."

Damn feet. His own ached like a son-of-a-bitch, too. Way to kill the mood.

"We can sit back down," he said, trying to keep the plea out of his voice.

Grace sighed. "I'd like to, but that's probably not a good idea."

"I think it's an excellent idea." Cade tucked a strand of hair behind her ear and smiled. He could see that logic had returned Grace to her usual equilibrium.

"With two gimped-up feet between us? Besides— " she placed a hand on Cade's chest, and when he covered hers with his, she stared at their hands.

"Besides?" he prompted, slowly letting go of the plans his other brain had made for the night.

"Besides, we barely know each other." The apology in her eyes cemented things for him. "I need more time, Cade."

With a gulp that buried the deep sigh he wanted to breathe out, Cade reached for her shoulders, rubbing up and down her arms a few times before stepping back. "I'm in this for the long haul, beautiful. So you take all the time you need."

Grace's eyes misted over again, and she shook her head, keeping the tears at bay. "You're too good to me, Cade Huntington."

"Just going with the flow that feels right," he said. Better to keep it light than to delve into how deeply he'd begun to feel about this woman. Somehow, she'd wound herself around his heart. His head, too. He couldn't stop thinking about her.

"Come on, doctor," he said, reaching for her coat. "I'll limp you to your car."

He held her coat while she put it on, then grabbed his crutches, holding one out to her. When she shook her head, he chuckled.

"I know what my body can take," she said, smiling.

Cade's comeback died in his throat as the vision of her body and what he wanted it to take filled him with desire. Grace's hazel eyes widened then darkened. He dared to hope she felt the same need, but it wasn't the time. Before he stepped toward her, Cade turned and hobbled to the front door.

Once she was in her car, he leaned in, kissing her with gentle promise. "We've only just begun."

She smiled. "I sincerely hope so."

As she pulled away, Cade stood there in the middle of the street. She'd definitely wrapped herself around him in ways no woman had ever done before. For the first time in his life, Cade wanted more than a fling. He wanted the real thing. With Grace.

He hobbled back into the house, locked it up, and turned out all the holiday and house lights. Heading upstairs to his bathroom, he stripped, turning the shower to cold before he stepped in.

Chapter Eight

Day shift shouldn't be this busy. It was 2 p.m. and Grace hadn't stopped since her 7 a.m. arrival. How could a small town have so many problems? She stuck an errant lock of hair back into the bun at the nape of her neck and leaned on the counter at the med station. Her foot, which had felt fine this morning, now throbbed, even after two ibuprofen. And switching from days to nights and back again had wreaked havoc on her body.

"What's next, Stan?" Stan Nelson was just about the best ER nurse Grace had ever worked with. Plus, he didn't consider her the Ice Queen. They got along pretty well.

He pursed his lips. "I almost don't want to say."

"Can it be that bad?"

"No. Not at all. I just don't want to jinx us."

Anyone who'd ever worked in an emergency room knew the superstition. Mention that things are quiet and they won't be for long. Grace nodded and smiled. "I'll be in the breakroom."

"Good, because I forgot to tell you someone's waiting there for you."

"For me?" No one visited her at work. "Who?"

Stan grinned. "I'm not supposed to tell. Now get along. I'll come get you if something comes up."

Frowning, Grace reminded him to let her know when the MRI report was in for Mrs. Johnson, then headed down the hall with trepidation. Who was here? The first thing that hit her when she opened the door was the smell of something really delicious. Then she saw Cade's dancing brown eyes.

"You said you rarely ate anything healthy at work, so I thought I'd bring something in for you. Save you from those dastardly snack machines." He held out an upholstered chrome chair.

"You do know by now that I don't like surprises."

His smile faltered, but only for a moment. "This one, you'll like."

Shaking her head, Grace took the proffered seat. "Is this going to be what life with you is like?"

"I hope so," Cade said, taking the seat next to her instead of across the table.

Way too close for Grace's sense of equilibrium.

"I'm happy you're thinking about life with me, though," Cade said, unpacking real silverware and plates.

Grace blushed, something she rarely did. And wouldn't you know it, at that moment, one of the nurses who thought of her as the Ice Queen came into the lounge. Grace didn't show emotion at work, at least not what she truly felt. And this was exactly why. The hospital was a gossip mecca and this nurse's eyes were wide open. Grace glared at her.

"Umm, I'll just come back later," the nurse said, scooting out as quickly as she'd entered.

Cade watched the woman back out of the room, then turned to Grace. "You use that look a lot? Because it's damn effective."

Emotion disrupted everything and right now, Grace couldn't stand that Cade had seen that side of her. Once he got to know her, he'd see that she really was the Ice Queen and disappear. She had faults, just like anyone else, but she'd be damned if she'd apologize for them. "I'm sorry," she said, standing. "This wasn't a good idea."

He reached for her hand. "Don't go."

Against her better wishes, she let herself be tugged back down to the chair.

"I didn't mean anything by my comment except admiration. I wish I could instigate action with a look."

"I need to be professional at work or I'll lose the respect of those I need to make hustle when hustle is needed. This"—she waved at the table—"doesn't help."

The way Cade ran his thumb over her hand distracted Grace, made her forget her train of thought.

"It's only lunch, Grace."

"Then why are you holding my hand?"

"Because I really like holding it." He grinned and let go. Grace had to admit she missed the contact.

"Come on, time to eat," he said. "Then I'll leave and let you go back to being the professional ER doc I respect and admire."

The food really did smell scrumptious. Some sort of salad with a wonderful, yeasty-smelling bread. "What is the salad?"

"A concoction chock full of good stuff that tastes great. Quinoa, black beans, garbanzo beans, tomatoes, cilantro, and a few other things, including my own signature dressing. Try it."

Grace generally ate the same thing and didn't experiment much, so she took a bite with no small amount of trepidation. "Wow," she said, letting the flavors float across her tongue. "This is really good."

"Don't sound so surprised."

"I'm not. I mean, I know you can cook. I'm just... not much of an experimenter."

"Oh, ho," Cade said, swallowing his own bite. "That's tantamount to throwing down the gauntlet for me. I'm looking forward to opening your eyes to a lot of new taste sensations."

She should have known not to give him anything even close to a dare. She shook her head and gave in gracefully. "Well, if your future food plans taste as good as this, we might get along just fine."

With a gleam in his eye, Cade leaned closer. "Trust me, Grace. We're going to get along better than fine."

The warmth that suffused Grace had nothing to do with embarrassment and everything to do with the promise in Cade's eyes.

"Your parents will love us being together," she said.

Cade sat back with a grimace. Grace was sorry she'd brought it up. Their closeness dissipated. "I don't really care what my parents think."

"I know. I shouldn't have said that."

"Mom has called me a couple times asking me to bring you to dinner."

"And you refused?"

"Yes." Cade reached to reclaim her hand. "I'd like to spend some time getting to know each other before my parents start trying to interfere."

"I get that. But Cade?"

"Uh-huh?"

She smiled, noticing how distracted he was gazing at their entwined hands.

"When you're ready, I'm okay going to your parents for dinner. I can handle them."

He frowned. "It would get them off my back."

"Then why not schedule something? Get it over with. I've already met them. Seems like an evening with them is a small price to pay for your sanity." She truly didn't think it would be that bad.

"All right. I'll set something up." The resignation in

his voice almost made Grace laugh.

"Dr. Benson?"

Grace whipped around, grateful the person speaking was the one person here who liked her. "Yes, Stan?"

"New patient, urgent, but not emergent."

Which was their code for not life-threatening, but needing quick attention. Grace stood and looked at Cade.

"Go," he said. "I'll leave your lunch in the fridge over there."

Nodding her gratitude, she followed Stan out. Once the breakroom door closed behind them, Grace let regret over the interrupted lunch settle for just a moment, then switched gears. From girlfriend to doctor. Stan handed her a chart as they rushed to the room. "Car accident. It looks like an open tib/fib fracture."

After assessing the patient and ordering pain meds and X-rays, Grace returned to the lounge, half hoping Cade would still be there. She missed him already and she appreciated the way he'd acknowledged the importance of her job and wrapped up her lunch for her. Another point in his favor. She found the salad in the fridge. When she opened the Styrofoam lid, Cade had drawn a heart on the inside of it. Not outside where everyone could see, but inside, for her eyes only.

She dug in, unable to wipe the smile from her face over Cade's efforts to make her feel as comfortable as possible. And to leave her well-fed, as the salad was superb. The bread filled her with thoughts of her father, who'd never been much of a cook but loved to bake.

Today was a good day. A very good one.

~ ~ ~

Distasteful stuff always came first on Cade's to-do list, which was why, when his parents suggested the next night for dinner, he'd agreed. Better to get it over with.

Cade pulled up in front of Grace's house with no small amount of trepidation, at least until he saw her waiting for him on the sidewalk. She hopped in before he could get out to help her.

"Thought I'd save you from grabbing a crutch," Grace said.

She settled into her seat and hesitated before leaning in for his kiss. "Speaking of which, how's the ankle feeling?"

"A lot better. Little or no pain and I'm off the ibuprofen."

"Good. You can try going without the crutches starting tomorrow. It'll be a week since you sprained it."

"Thank God." He'd be more than happy to ditch the damn things. "Hey, you're not hobbling."

"I bounce back quickly from these things."

Grace laughed and Cade drank in the happy sound. Being with Grace made everything enjoyable. With her along, he didn't completely dread tonight's dinner. He leaned over the console and kissed her.

"You look lovely, Grace," he said, though he couldn't see what she wore beyond dark slacks and a camel-colored long coat. She'd left her hair down and he wanted to run his hands through the thick, wavy blonde tresses. "No scrubs, huh? How did you have time?"

I didn't think scrubs would be appropriate for dinner with your parents, so I freshened up and changed at the hospital."

He looked down at his jeans, making sure he'd changed out of the ripped ones. He had. "They do like a touch of formality. Thanks for going with me. I'll be glad to get this over with."

Cade's parents lived further up the beach from Willow Bay, so it was close to 8 p.m. when they arrived.

"Are you sure your parents don't mind the late dinner?"

"They're so giddy with plans for you, they wouldn't mind if it was midnight."

As Cade moved to exit his SUV, Grace stilled him with a hand on his arm. "Just so you know, I know my own mind. I know what I want and don't want, and I can hold my own with your parents. Don't worry about tonight."

Stuck on her words, "I know what I want," Cade barely caught the rest of her story. He hoped and prayed she wanted him. But first, they had dinner to get through. "I'll try my best," he said.

After helping her out of his rig, they headed towards the open front door. His parents stood on the porch with wide smiles on their faces. This was so not going to be fun.

"Dr. Benson, it's lovely to see you again." Cade's mother gave Grace a light hug, then turned her cheek up for Cade's peck.

"Call me Grace, please, and I hope I may call you Michelle and Lawrence."

Round one to Grace, Cade thought as he shook his father's hand. His parents preferred to be called by their degrees.

"Of course, Grace. Our given names will be fine. Come in, come in. It's way too chilly to be standing out here on the porch."

After they doffed their coats, Cade led Grace into the great room, grimacing when he saw the table set with his parents' very best china, edged in gold. And crystal goblets and—he tried to count from where he stood—six different types of silverware.

"Mom, it's late. You didn't have to go to all this trouble."

"Yes, I'm so sorry we're so late. You know hospital shifts, though," Grace added.

"We didn't go to any trouble, and the time is fine.

Dr., er, Lawrence and I generally eat late anyway. We did keep it to a lighter fare, though, so you wouldn't go home with an overfull stomach. Some of those meals Cade makes can sit for hours without being digested."

Really? The first thing she does is insult his cooking? She'd rarely eaten his food, mostly because Cade didn't invite them over. The hit of guilt surprised him and he quickly buried it.

"Oh, Cade cooked for me the other night and it was wonderful."

He grinned and put his arm around Grace's waist. "I'll cook for you any day."

"Well," Cade's mother said with a pointed stare at him. "Maybe we need to try his cooking again."

No way in hell was he inviting them over right now. One meal a month was about all he could stomach.

"Can I get you something to drink?" his father asked.

"Just water for me," Grace said.

"Same," Cade echoed.

"Water for everyone, then," his mother said, pulling Grace toward the table.

"So, tell me why you chose emergency room work," his mother said as they all sat down.

The soup and salad courses passed with more than one innuendo about clinic work versus emergency room work. During the main course—salmon with a pistachio rub that had Cade asking cook for the recipe—his parents upped their game.

"You know, I'm a little out of the loop on hospital pay," his father said to Grace. "But I have to believe it would be more lucrative for you in a clinic setting like ours."

"Dad, stop hounding her."

Grace turned her best "I've got this" gaze to Cade, then looked at both his parents. "I'm sure it would, if I was driven by money."

"What does drive you?" Cade's mother asked.

With a deep breath, Grace sat back. "I like triage and I'm good at it, so ER work suits me."

"Oh, there's a lot of triage at the clinic. Why just yesterday, we had to send Jim Henderson on to your hospital after he came in spouting about the worst pain ever. We knew it was gallstones. Turns out we were right."

"I'm aware you'd like to convert me to a clinical doctor." Grace turned a disarming smile on them both. "I hope you'll respect that my choice, for the moment, is to remain at Grays Harbor General. I promise you, if I ever change my mind and want that small-town clinic feel, you'll be the"—she glanced at Cade—"third and fourth persons to know."

That's my girl. "Hopefully now, dear parents, we can put this whole head-hunting thing to rest?

Though they didn't look pleased, his parents miraculously let the subject drop and dessert passed without incident. After saying their goodbyes and climbing back into his SUV, Cade let out a long sigh.

"I'm sorry about my parents."

"They are persistent, that's for certain. But it's nothing I can't handle."

"You shut them down perfectly, showing respect yet making it clear you were not in the market for the job they were offering. I wish I could deal with them so easily."

"I do sense a lot of tension between the three of you."

"Yes. I think, because I'm an only child, they'd planned their lives around mine. When I didn't go in the direction they wanted, it threw them for a loop. I get it. And at first, I tried to be understanding."

"How long has it been since you left med school?"

"Ummm, eight years, or thereabouts. They like to dig at my life, so I just stopped caring. A long time ago."

"I can understand that."

Grace's wistful tone made Cade instantly sorry. "You shouldn't have to deal with my folks after what you've gone through."

"You know, I always thought I'd missed out, not having a complete family." She shook her head and a quick smile touched her face. "You've shown me a different side of family life. Still, I think you're lucky."

He reached for her hand. "Deep down inside, I agree with you. I am lucky. I had a great upbringing and didn't have to deal with trauma like you."

When they reached Grace's house, Cade walked her to her door and kissed her goodnight, a lingering kiss that he didn't want to end. "You're tired, I know." Maybe she'd invite him in anyhow.

"I am."

Well, damn. Cade sighed and tugged on a strand of her hair. "Sleep well, Dr. Grace. Dream of me."

"Not conducive to a good night's sleep," she said, leaning against him. "But I probably will."

He waited until she'd locked the door behind her. As he walked to his SUV, he realized he hadn't used his crutches all night and his foot wasn't throbbing. It was sore, but not too bad. He'd go home and ice it, take a cool shower, and then find Grace in his dreams.

Chapter Nine

Sunday night, Cade stepped back from his standing desk, content with the amount of work he'd accomplished on a new gaming concept. He looked forward to pitching it at the next conference, but there was still a lot to do. He had three months. It was enough, but Cade decided he'd better call his agent and get him working on some buzz about it.

Heading downstairs sans crutches, he opened the fridge and pulled out a water, glancing at the clock. 7:30 p.m. Grace should be off work by now. He'd give her an hour, then call. Twelve-hour shifts had to wear a person out, especially when those shifts came four days in a row. She had to be exhausted. He might be able to pull those hours, but he admired the hell out of Grace, not only for the hours she put in, but for the life and death decisions she made daily. Way beyond his abilities and a big part of the reason he hadn't followed in his parents' footsteps.

He took some leftovers from the fridge and set them to heat up just as his phone rang. Grace. Punching the stop button on the microwave, he answered the phone.

"Hello, gorgeous."

"Hi, Cade."

She sounded about dead on her feet.

"This is a nice surprise. Done with your shift?"

"Yes. I'm on my way home. Didn't want to fall asleep at the wheel so I thought maybe you could keep me awake until I got home."

"I'd be happy to. How was your day?"

"Good. I got to deliver a baby. That doesn't happen often in the ER, but that little girl was waiting for no one."

"I can't even imagine bringing a child into the world like that. I can imagine making them, though."

"A little focused on sex, are you?"

He could hear the laughter in her voice. He'd distracted her, made her smile. That pleased him to no end.

"Well, when I'm spending my nights taking cold showers—"

"You aren't!" she said.

"You, Dr. Grace, underestimate your allure."

"I— shit!"

Screeching tires screamed through the phone at Cade. "Grace? What's wrong? What happened?"

For way too long, all he heard was heavy breathing. At least it was breathing. "Grace? What happened?"

"I'm okay, Cade." Grace's voice was tense but got stronger as she continued. "There's been an accident. I'm okay, but I have to go."

The call disconnected and Cade stared at his phone for a long moment, his heart in his throat. She'd disconnected, not the car. She really was okay. Cade kept telling himself that over and over as he grabbed his keys and raced for his SUV, grateful he wasn't in that damn boot any longer. Barely a twinge to the ankle, thank goodness.

Halfway out of town, he fell in behind the Willow Bay sheriff's cruiser. Cade didn't give a thought to speed. He just followed, knowing the only police car in Willow Bay would lead him to the accident. Sure enough, in five minutes they found the grisly scene. An RV lay on its mangled side, the cab almost unrecognizable. On the opposite side of the road, a box truck canted over the edge with something lodged beneath it. Cade squinted. Was that a car?

Red, blue, and white lights flashed off the trees, lending a macabre tone to an already bad scene. Fire and ambulance had arrived. Cade leaped out of his car, closest to the box truck. He found Grace with half her body stuck inside the flattened car. Relief that she seemed okay warred with the danger he sensed as the box truck wobbled, half over the embankment.

"Grace!" He raced to her, grabbing her hips in the hopes it would keep her from going with the truck if it tumbled over the side.

She yelped and pulled out of the car, whirling on him. "Damn, Cade, don't scare me like that."

"I won't scare you if you don't scare me. This thing could topple at any moment."

"I was as safe as I could be." She frowned as she glanced at the mangled car. "Needed to be sure. This one didn't make it."

Damn. "How about the box truck driver?"

"Not too badly injured. He's over at the paramedics' rig."

"And the RV?" Personal belongings were everywhere, flung like a tornado had caught them.

"Whole family's alive. A miracle, too. Dad got the worst of it." Grace raced back around the RV ruins. Cade followed like a puppy on a leash. His heart might have been in his throat, worried about Grace, but this was her element and she'd taken command.

Two adults and two children, a boy and a girl, both of whom appeared to be under ten. The paramedics were working on the father. Mom sat between her two children holding an arm to her chest. Both kids lay on stretchers like their dad, but both were talking and crying, so that had to be good.

"Distract the family," Grace told Cade, rushing to where the father lay on a backboard with the crew working on him.

Distract the family? How the hell was he supposed to do that?

Cade hunkered down in front of them. "You all okay?"

With a shaky voice, the mother answered. "I think so. We're worried about Phil. Is he okay?"

Both kids, tears crawling down their cheeks, glanced at the activity behind Cade.

"I don't know," he said. "I'm not a paramedic. But the lady there"—he pointed at Grace—"she's an emergency room doctor at Grays Harbor General. So your guy's in good hands."

Someone handed a blanket over his shoulder and he wrapped it around the mother. They all heard Grace's next orders.

"All right. He's stabilized, but he hasn't regained consciousness. We need to get him to the hospital now. Get him loaded up and head out. I'll call ahead and warn them he might need to be medevaced to Harborview."

No one argued with her orders. The injured man was on his way in seconds. Cade helped the mother and kids into the second ambulance, and the driver of the box truck left in the last one.

Jackson Smith, Willow Bay's sheriff, came up to them. "We'll take care of this mess. When the fire department retrieves the body from the car, we'll send it on to the Grays Harbor morgue."

"That's fine," Grace said. "I need to get to the hospital."

"I'll drive you," Cade said.

"I can drive myself."

"You can be on the phone while I drive you, then I'll bring you back to your car."

With a clipped nod, Grace headed for Cade's truck. He followed, waved to Jackson, and hopped in. Grace was already on her phone.

They caught up with the ambulances, getting to Grays Harbor in record time. Grace flew out of the car and into the emergency room. Cade parked and headed in more slowly. There wasn't much he could do, but he was glad he'd been able to help in some small way. And, this way he could make sure Grace got some food in her system. Cade settled in the ER waiting room for the long haul.

~~~

Moving her neck from side to side, Grace tried to loosen tight muscles. It had been a long four days, made even longer by tonight's accident, and she was beyond exhaustion. She headed for the door, then remembered her car wasn't in the parking lot. Diverting to the waiting room, she found Cade sound asleep in one of the chairs. Grace sank onto the chair next to him, observing his peaceful slumber. The sharp angle of his head didn't look all that comfortable, yet a smile touched his face, just at the corner of a very kissable mouth. She liked his dark beard even though it was thicker than she was used to. Grace reached out and ran her hand along the coarse hair, enjoying the feel of it.

When Cade's sleep-filled eyes opened, his smile widened. Grace forgot all about her fatigue as she smiled back.

"Ready to go home, beautiful?" he asked in a husky, just-woke-up voice that made her tingle in places she'd ignored for far too long.

Grace nodded, pulling her hand away from his beard. Cade reached for it, engulfing it in his. "Then let's get outta here." He stood, pulling her with him, his eyes telling her he wanted to pull her in close. Instead, he glanced around, then headed for the exit. In the parking lot, he leaned her back against his truck and put a hand on either side, trapping her. Yet Grace didn't feel trapped. She wanted to be close to Cade, closer even than they were now.

So much closer. And she wanted it more than anything.

"Do you know how hot you are when you do that take-charge thing like you did at the accident?" he asked, his voice still husky.

When his lips claimed hers, she gave herself over to the sensations. Emotion swirled, need coursed, and desire shot straight to her core. She reveled in his touch. He made her feel sexy, full of life, worthy—a heady mixture. She tangled her fingers in his hair and brought him in closer. Tighter.

The kiss left them both breathing hard.

"Damn, what you do to me, woman."

"What I do to you? My whole body is shaking."

Grinning, Cade opened the door for her. "That might actually be a lack of food."

"This has nothing to do with food," Grace said, pulling him close for another kiss.

When she let him go, his smokey brown eyes stared at her for a long moment, dipping to lips well-kissed, then back to her eyes. He closed her door quietly and went around to get in the driver's seat. Once settled, he placed an arm along the back of her seat.

"As much as I'd like to head straight for a bed and continue this discussion, I think you need some food and some sleep first."

The adrenaline surge from the accident and Cade's kiss had peaked and was now heading for a cliff. Grace sank back into the seat, resting her head. "You might be right."

"How about we pick up some takeout and head back to your place."

"Cade— " God, she wanted him. But could she handle it right now? Probably not.

"Don't worry. I don't molest exhausted women." He leaned in closer. "When we make love, I want us both refreshed." His eyes sparkled with dark desire. "We're going to need that energy."

Her breath hitched, thinking about Cade, in bed, naked, with her.

"Tonight, it's food and sleep."

Grace nodded. Even though she wanted more, Cade was right. Sleep first. As he pulled out of the hospital parking lot, she closed her eyes and drifted off, more than willing to turn everything over to him for now.

Chapter Ten

Outside Grace's house, Cade shut off the engine and watched Grace. She'd slept through him handing her car keys to Jackson, the sheriff, who said he would deliver her car to the house in the morning. McDonald's had been the only place open to get food. As much as he preferred home-cooked, this would have to do. Grace had slept through that as well.

At the accident, she'd been in her element, even with one death weighing her down. He'd been completely wowed seeing her in action. Grace Benson was an amazing woman and Cade knew, if things didn't work out between them, it would take him a long, long time to get past her. He'd fallen for this angel of mercy. Big time.

He got out of his SUV and went quietly around to her side. When he opened the door, she stirred. "Hey," he said. "We're home." He unbuckled her seatbelt and grabbed the sack of food.

Grace stumbled as they made their way to the front door. By the time he got them inside, Cade had realized Grace needed sleep more than food. He set the McDonald's bag down, keeping a watchful eye out for her cat.

"Where's your bedroom, darlin'?"

She pointed upstairs. When Cade picked her up, she didn't complain, just rested her head on his shoulder. Her trust wound around his heart with a warmth that drove him even further into the soul-mate realm. In the bedroom, he found Luna curled up in the middle of Grace's bed.

Using one arm to steady her, he set Grace on her feet then gingerly pulled back the covers.

"Your mistress is tired, Luna," he said in a soothing voice, hoping the cat would recognize that Cade had Grace's best interests at heart. Luna eyed him but didn't budge.

"Sit," he said to Grace.

"Shoes," she whispered.

"Got 'em." He slipped her shoes and socks off, then lifted her legs to help her lay down. She was in hospital scrubs. No reason she couldn't just sleep in them. Cade pulled the covers up around her chin and leaned down to kiss her on the forehead. "Get some sleep."

Her eyes barely open, Grace reached up and pulled him in for a kiss. "Thank you. For everything." She let him go and snuggled deeper under the blanket with a gentle sigh that softened Cade's heart even further. Luna sat up, stretched, and moved to cuddle against Grace's side. Lucky cat.

Cade turned the light off and pulled the door mostly closed, knowing that he was sunk. And happy to be there.

~~~

Grace woke slowly, comfortable and warm in her own bed, but not completely sure how she'd gotten there. Her phone, sitting on the nightstand, said 4:30. Still dark out, and she hadn't left the hospital until midnight. With Cade.

She shot up and looked around. No Cade. He'd brought her home. That much, she remembered. Climbing out of bed, she went to the window. His SUV and hers were parked outside. How had he gotten her car home?

Shivering in the coolness, Grace realized she was still in scrubs. And boy, did she need a shower. But first, she needed more sleep, and she wouldn't get that until she found Cade.

A few minutes later, she spotted him on the couch, curled up because it wasn't long enough for his frame, and covered by the afghan that usually lay over the back of it. Luna was snugged between the crook of Cade's legs and the couch back.

"So you've decided you like him then?" Grace whispered, watching Cade. He looked neither comfortable nor warm. But cuter than any man had a right to look.

"Cade," she said, gently shaking him. "Come to bed."

He opened his eyes, but they remained glassy. "Come on," Grace said, pulling on his hand. "Let's get you more comfortable."

When he unfolded from the couch in nothing but boxers, Grace gulped. He had the physique of a man who worked out regularly and she wanted to run her hands over the muscles flexing across his stomach. But not now. Tired still won the moment.

"Come on. Let's go to bed."

Somehow, they made it up the stairs. Unsure if Cade was awake enough to know where he was, Grace put him in bed, changed into a t-shirt and shorts, slid in beside him and pulled- the covers up, prepared to turn away from him and go back to sleep.

"Come here," he said, his voice husky. "I want to sleep with you in my arms."

Grace curled into his side, exactly where she wanted to be. They fit together perfectly and she snuggled in deeper, causing Cade to sigh and tighten his arm around her.

"You feel good."

So did he, she thought, closing her eyes, though sleep did not come right away. She'd never slept with a man. At least, not like this. It surprised her that she didn't feel uncomfortable. In fact, it felt more than comfortable. It felt right. Grace closed her eyes, wondering why that didn't scare her.

Chapter Eleven

Grace woke to daylight streaming through the windows and gentle snores coming from the chest beneath her hand, rising and falling with regularity. Cade. Her head lay on his shoulder, his arm still around her. Grace smiled and wondered why she'd never had a man sleep over before. Except, she knew why. It had never felt right. Her smile faltered. Was she ready for this?

She realized her leg was boldly thrown over Cade. In fact, his reaction lay beneath her leg, hard and ready.

"Good morning, darlin'."

"H-hi." Grace ducked her head into his chest and tried to move her leg.

Cade's hand, which rested on said leg, tightened. "Not quite yet. This feels way too good for us to be moving."

"But— You— "

"Have a morning boner? Sure do."

Grace tried not to smile but the edge of laughter in Cade's voice didn't make it easy. And the circles his finger made along the back of her knee didn't help.

"Kiss me," he said.

"No." Grace covered her mouth.

"Why not?"

"Morning breath."

"I don't care. Kiss me."

"Cade— "

His hand stopped doing those lazy trails along her leg as he reached to tip her chin up. His eyes, dark smoke and desire, crinkled at the corners. "Kiss me."

How could she refuse? Grace pressed her lips to his. Any thought of morning breath disappeared with that first touch. Her mind filled with Cade, his touch, his gentleness, his caring. His lips moved over hers like a caress and her body responded.

Cade tightened his hold. At the same time, his stomach growled—loud and long—breaking the moment. They chuckled, even as they held onto each other like nothing else mattered.

"Guess we'd better eat before we do anything else?"

"Well, that growl of yours might be a touch distracting in the midst of, well, you know."

"Making love, Grace. That's what we'll be doing. Making love. Say it."

She'd never been with a man like Cade. He made her forget everything except the overwhelming need to be with him. Grace did not use the "L" word easily, especially when it came to sex with someone she had feelings for that she couldn't quite define.

He watched her quietly, adding to the pressure.

"Not quite ready for that." A slice of honesty, without making the deep dive into emotional territory.

Cade threw his head back and laughed. "That's one of the things I lo—like so much about you, Grace. Your honesty. Okay, then." He leaped out of bed, holding out his hand. "Breakfast it is."

What a magnificent body Cade had. Standing there in his boxer shorts, displaying those six-pack abs with that boyish grin on his face, Grace was tempted to toss breakfast out the door and haul him back to bed. Very tempted. Putting a hand over her heart to slow it the hell down, she reached for his hand.

"You're tempted, aren't you?" His voice, low and inviting, sang to parts of Grace that had lain dormant for way too long. He pulled her out of bed and into his arms.

Grace nodded and touched his beard. "I'm not sure I'm ready for you, Cade Huntington."

"I'm not sure you are, either."

She slapped his shoulder and he laughed, kissing her lightly. "Come on, let's see what you have in this house for breakfast."

~~~

Cade rooted through Grace's refrigerator while she fed the cat, who seemed to have decided Cade was a friendly. "You've got a lot of good stuff in here." Hand full, he turned to the kitchen island and set everything down.

As she moved to the coffeemaker, Grace chuckled. "I do try to eat healthy once in a while."

She pulled cups from the cupboard. "Cream? Sugar?"

"Black and leaded," Cade said, clearing his dry throat. He'd almost missed the question, distracted by the sight of her moving around in a not-quite-loose t-shirt and sleep shorts. He imagined her making coffee with nothing on.

Grace moved past him, shutting his mouth with a finger under his chin. "You went there again, didn't you?"

He stopped her and pulled her into his arms. "Where you're concerned, I always go there."

Her eyes darkened as she cupped his chin. "You say the nicest things."

"Only to you." He meant it, too. Somehow, in the last few days, Cade had become a one-woman man.

"Breakfast first. And maybe some conversation. I don't feel like I know much about you," Grace said.

She reached to grab plates from the cupboard so he let her go. "Am I cooking or are you?" she asked.

A lovesick puppy. Cade knew that's what he must look like. Damn, but he had it bad. He turned back to the island. "I'm cooking."

In no time, he'd whipped up vegetarian omelets and sliced cantaloupe. They took everything to the table and sat just as his stomach let out another loud growl.

"Food first, then talk," Cade said.

"Definitely."

He took a bite, then sat back to chew it. Grace took a bite and the evident joy on her face made him feel good. He could cook well and considered himself a bit of a connoisseur, but whether or not people liked his tastes was something he couldn't control. Like his parents, who found fault with his cooking, and just about everything else.

"This is exceptional, Cade," Grace said when she'd finished the bite. "I can't believe you made this with stuff from my kitchen."

While Cade never tried to live up to others' expectations of him, damned if he didn't go all warm and fuzzy inside at her compliment. "You had seasonings I liked."

"But I'd never think of putting leftover lentils in an omelet. With the spinach and the seasoning, it melts in my mouth."

Speaking of her mouth, he wanted to kiss her again more than anything. To shove the food aside and lay her on this table and show her how much she meant to him.

"Cade, you're doing it again."

He shook his head to clear it. "Well, not going to apologize. You make me think dangerous things."

"We need safer territory. How did you learn to cook

so well?"

"Self-preservation. With two doctors as parents, they were gone more than they were home." He held up a hand at the concern on her face. "Don't worry. I had a great childhood and they made sure I felt loved. But if I wanted to eat decent food, I had to learn to make it myself. Turns out, I enjoy cooking."

"And you're very good at it. You can cook for me anytime."

"I'm going to hold you to that statement."

"I'm going to let you." Grace grinned, distracting him with the way she chewed her cantaloupe. "So, both parents are doctors. How come you didn't follow suit?"

Cade tried not to stiffen. This letting-the-folks-down thing was uncomfortable territory. But Grace had gifted him with her story, so she deserved honesty from him. Though the secret he held grated at him. He needed to tell her about his true profession, and just how much he earned doing it. Should he do it now? He decided to work up to it.

"I tried med school. I started college with that in mind." He looked out her window at the rain. "It just wasn't my thing. I was unhappy and I started drinking too much. That's why I don't drink much at all now. I didn't like who I was becoming. So I gave up on med school, let my parents down, and that's about it."

"That couldn't have been easy, telling them you weren't going to follow in their footsteps."

"It's still a bone of contention between us. They are bitterly disappointed."

Grace pointed her fork at him. "Yes, I got that impression. And now, they're full of hope that you'll somehow bring them a doctor."

He nodded as Grace looked around her kitchen. "Your place is pretty modern compared to mine."

Noting the change of subject, Cade wondered if

she'd done that for him, or was this touchy territory for her? "I like your house," he said. "It's homey and traditional."

"Except it's missing Christmas, right?"

"Well, there is that." He grinned. "Seriously, though, it's got great bones."

"I have plans to modern it up a bit, but not too much. I hate it when people paint beautiful wood trim."

"I agree."

Grace looked at him, a question on her face. "I still wonder how you can afford that house of yours on a cable installer's salary."

Here we go. Time to 'fess up and take the hits. Cade's hands went clammy and he rubbed them on his jeans under the table. He didn't know what he'd do if Grace put an end to them. But damn, she deserved to know everything about him. He wanted her to know. He just didn't want her to disappear because of it.

"There's more to me than hooking up televisions."

"Oh, I don't doubt— " Grace stopped as her ever-present phone pinged. She glanced at it, then back up at Cade, apology in her eyes. "I'm so sorry. I just got called into work. They're overloaded."

Was it horrible that Cade felt an overwhelming sense of relief? He shoved it all aside and focused on Grace. "What can I do to get you on your way?"

"If you can take care of clean up and lock the house after you, I'll just dress and head out." She stood, taking her dishes to the sink.

"Done." Cade rounded the island and pulled her into his arms, kissing her with a promise he wanted very badly to keep.

"I'm sorry," she said. "I really wanted to spend this day with you." She glanced toward the stairs, then back at Cade. "In bed."

"Oh, me, too, darlin'. Me, too. But we'll have our

moment. Now go get ready." He backed up, giving her a gentle swat on the butt, making her yelp. Her laughter followed her up the stairs and Cade stood there reveling in the moment. He turned on the water to rinse dishes, knowing he had to come clean before they made love. If Grace felt betrayed by lies, she'd feel he took advantage of her, and she'd be right. And, since she wasn't a rip-the-bandage-off kind of person, this would take some finesse.

After Grace left, he finished the dishes and wandered around her main room for a bit. He liked the place. Built-in bookcases and a wide, natural wood mantel framed a newer gas fireplace. The original red brick stood out against the white. Would she want to tile this?

He sat on the couch and Luna, loud purr and all, jumped in his lap and rubbed up against him.

"Yep. We're definitely buddies now, aren't we?" Cade said, scratching behind Luna's ear. A book on the coffee table caught his attention and he picked it up, flipping it over to read the blurb. A medical mystery. Made sense.

His phone beeped and he glanced at the text asking if he could take on a cable install this afternoon. He could now, he thought with regret. Locking up the house, he hopped in his truck and headed for home and a shower, vowing to have a long talk with Grace at the earliest convenience. He wanted her to love all of him like he loved her, and that meant coming clean.

Chapter Twelve

Grace stepped out of the shower and dried off, feeling human again. After she was called into the hospital because of an overloaded ER and a sick doctor, she'd handled a full twelve-hour shift. So officially, she'd now worked five twelve-hour shifts in a row. She'd been so rummy last night, she'd asked Cade to come drive her home.

Which he'd gladly done. Then, being the amazing man he was, he'd kissed her with tender care at her front door and left her to sleep. She'd almost invited him in, but he'd known she needed to be alone, to recover. The man had the most astounding intuition.

Calling him last night had filled her with warm fuzzies. Grace had never had someone in her life to help when she'd pushed herself beyond what she could handle. It was nice. Everything about Cade felt nice. Good. Amazing. And being close to him, sleeping with him, kissing him... Her body heated up just thinking about it.

Today, she would not be going to work. Hospital admin had demanded she take two days off. They'd brought in a physician from Olympia to cover, so she had two glorious days free before her shift on the twenty-third. And, for the first time in her life, she had Christmas Eve and Christmas off due to the long hours she'd been putting in. Grace had always worked Christmas. It was so much better than being home alone with her thoughts. She'd planned to do the same this year until the hospital insisted she take some days off.

Grace swallowed, trying to dislodge the worry stuck in her throat. She'd spent years burying all the hurt, all the feelings of inadequacy. Would having Christmas off give her too much time to wallow in a vat of self-pity? She hated that idea. She'd worked too hard to keep that fear and worry at bay.

Maybe this year, she could be with Cade. It might add a level of happiness to the holiday that was foreign to Grace. She didn't know how she felt about it, but she forced her thoughts in another direction. Cade would be here in about an hour to take her to get her SUV. She hoped they could spend these next two days together. If he didn't have to work. She hadn't asked him.

Pulling on her bathrobe, she went to get dressed. As far as she could tell, Cade's job was amazingly flexible. He never seemed to be out doing an installation when she called and they'd spent some time together during business hours. She'd have to ask him about that too. How did he fit work into his life?

After sex. She'd ask him after sex, because that was the main thing on her mind right now. She'd waited too long and refused to wait a single day more. Which was why she'd taken extra time to primp in the shower. And now she picked out comfortable but body-molded jeans and her softest, clingiest sweater. She planned to make sure Cade was in the mood today, though she doubted that would be a problem based on how he looked at her. Like a hungry tiger ready to claim his dinner.

Did she look at him the same way? Probably.

Smiling, she dressed and headed back into the bathroom to put on her makeup. She spritzed with a light, airy perfume she rarely got to wear, then wondered if Cade had any allergy or asthma issues. Better to err on the side of caution. She grabbed a washcloth and wiped it off.

The doorbell rang just as she was slipping into her shoes.

"Hello, darlin'." Cade leaned against the doorframe and eyed her up and down, appreciation in his smoldering eyes. "Wow."

She could say the same thing. He wore jeans that highlighted his muscular thighs, a white, button-up shirt, and a long, black peacoat. The shirt was untucked and the first few buttons were undone, offering a tantalizing glimpse of his chest. He looked amazing. His hair, its normal organized mess, begged to have her hands running through it.

"Yes," Grace said, clearing her throat. "Wow."

His grin widened. "Ready to enjoy the day?"

"Definitely. Just need to feed Luna." Grace made quick work of her cat chores, grabbed her coat and purse, and stepped outside, locking the door behind her. She slipped on the icy sidewalk and Cade caught her, taking advantage of their closeness to kiss her.

"Did you do that on purpose so I'd kiss you?"

"No!" Grace reddened, silently thanking Mother Nature for the assist. She'd worn sturdy tennies, but glancing down at Cade's hikers, she realized she should get something better suited to the winters here. She'd left most of her deep winter gear there thinking she wouldn't need it. Live and learn.

Cade helped her into his SUV, then hopped in on the other side.

"So what shall we do today?" he asked as he pulled out.

"Spend it together."

He grinned and grabbed her hand, settling it on his leg, keeping his warm, comfy hand on top of hers. "That's a given. Today, and if you'll have me, tonight and tomorrow." He spared a glance at her. From the intensity in his gaze, his desire matched her own.

"That's exactly what I was thinking."

"Good." He tightened his hold on her hand. "I love it when we're on the same page."

In what seemed like no time at all, they arrived at the hospital. Cade saw her to her car but didn't kiss her, though she could tell he wanted to.

"I'll follow you back to your house," he said.

The drive home was interminable. When she finally parked her car in the garage and climbed back into Cade's truck, he pulled her halfway across the console and kissed the life out of her. Grace kissed him right back.

"I missed you," he said against her lips.

"Mmmm. I missed you, too. And this." She renewed their kiss.

When they finally broke apart, Cade had to turn the defrost on full blast to clear the windows. "Been a lot of years since I had a make-out session in my rig. I don't remember them feeling this good. Ever."

"You do strange things to me, Cade Huntington." She ran her hand along his beard. She'd grown very fond of it and paused to imagine what it would feel like against her skin. And other parts.

"If you keep looking at me like that, I'll shut this car off and beg you to take me to your bedroom."

"Sounds like a perfect idea to me." Grace reached for her door handle, but Cade stopped her.

"Let's take our time. Make this last by spending the day together. I'll cook dinner at my place."

Grace chafed with impatience. Now that she'd made up her mind, she couldn't seem to think about anything but Cade. In bed. With her. The incentive of a night with

Cade made the wait tolerable, though. "Sounds lovely." She smiled, happy at Cade's wide grin when she accepted his idea.

"So what will we do today?" she asked.

"You haven't had much chance to really see Willow Bay, right?"

"Right. I've barely seen a thing."

"I thought I could show you the highlights. The lighthouse, a drive on the beach, and a walk if the weather allows. And maybe my teen make-out spot." He waggled his eyebrows and Grace laughed.

"If you're up for it, I thought we'd finish with a stroll after dark through Cannery Park."

Grace frowned. "Where they have all the Christmas lights strung over the pathways?"

He nodded. "Then we'll head to my place and I'll cook dinner. After which— "

Cade left the thought hanging, but a zing suffused Grace's entire body. She could handle a few holiday lights for that "after."

"Sounds good to me."

"Great. Let's get our day started."

~~~

Happy to find Luke's truck already parked at the lighthouse, Cade pulled up beside it. He was also relieved that the only Christmas decoration in sight was a wreath hanging on the lighthouse door. Baby steps.

Grace climbed out and craned her neck to look at the structure. "This is a lot bigger close-up."

"Wait until you see the view from the top."

"We can go inside?"

"Not everyone can, but the caretaker's a friend. Luke's a local construction guy who keeps the lighthouse in good shape and volunteered to give us a tour."

At that moment, Luke opened the door and beckoned them in. "Come on in out of the cold."

Once inside, they saw Gladys relaxing in a chair. They exchanged hellos.

"Luke was kind enough to offer me a place to rest for a few minutes." The speculation in Gladys's gaze when she grinned at them worried Cade. The old woman was up to something or thinking too much. Cade had the distinct feeling he and Grace were part of whatever plan she was hatching.

"How are you feeling, Gladys? Is this your usual tired or a new kind of tired?"

Always in doctor mode, his woman.

"I'm fine. Just warming up." Gladys never let a sign of weakness slip. One day, Cade hoped they'd learn her story. And get her to come in from the cold for more than just a quick warm-up.

Cade bit back his comment and introduced Grace to Luke.

"It's nice to meet you," Luke said. With a wide grin and a glance at Gladys that meant nothing but trouble, he added, "You must be someone special to this lug. He's never brought anyone around here before."

Yep, these two were up to no good, trying to butt into a relationship he could take care of on his own just fine.

Grace's luminous smile softened him. He gave in gracefully.

"You're right, Luke. She's special." He meant it, too. Big time.

While Gladys stayed put, the rest of them headed upstairs, where Luke showed them how the light worked before opening the door to the outer walkway. Grace went first. When a gust of wind blew her back into Cade's arms, he held her against him as they stepped outside, then leaned against the lighthouse wall so the wind couldn't get to her. Luke headed back downstairs. Smart man.

"This is beautiful," Grace said.

The ocean rolls crested a ways out, foaming as white spray raced to the shore. The sound, something Cade would never tire of, rumbled through and over them. Just then, the clouds gave way and sunshine sliced across the dark water, turning a swath into dancing sprites for a moment before disappearing.

"I never get tired of this view," he said, voicing his thoughts.

"I can see why."

When Grace turned her head to look back at him, Cade captured her mouth with his, emotions rolling through him and cresting like the waves. When she reached with an arm to tug him closer, deeper, Cade turned her in his arms, pouring all the love he felt into the kiss. She opened to him, tasted him as he tasted her, gave him everything and he took it.

She was heaven incarnate and he never wanted to leave this spot.

~~~

A blast of wind rounded the lighthouse and pulled the breath from Grace. She gasped at the cold, breaking the magic moment.

"Getting colder. We'd better go in," Cade said.

Grace snuggled into him for another moment before she could bring herself to let go.

"Don't worry," he said with a chuckle. "There will be a lot more kissing before this day is over."

"There'd better be."

Cade laughed out loud, holding the door for her. Inside, much warmer without the wind, they began the trek down the stairs when Cade's phone rang. Grace saw that it was his parents.

"You'd better answer it."

Glad when he accepted her request and answered, Grace moved away to give him some privacy.

"Hi, Mom."

"No, I'm not working."

"Yes, I'm with Grace."

"And no, we have plans tonight. Sorry."

It took a couple more minutes of convincing before he could disconnect. Grace couldn't stop the laughter that rumbled from her throat. "They wanted us to come over again, didn't they?"

"God, yes," Cade said, a pained expression on his face. "We were just there four days ago."

"I'll give them credit. They are persistent."

"That's the nice way of putting it. Let's get on with our day. I don't want to think about my folks one more minute. This day is all about us."

They traversed the stairs. "Gladys gone?"

"Yep," Luke said, putting some things in a box. "Said she'd seen what she came to see."

"I bet," Cade mumbled. "You moving out?"

He nodded.

"Luke maintains the lighthouse and stays here sometimes," Cade explained to Grace.

"Yes, but now that Jasmin and I are living together, I won't be sleeping here anymore."

The joy on Luke's face made Grace wonder if she'd ever look that happy. Be that happy.

"I'm glad for you, man. You and Jazz belong together." Cade shook Luke's hand, they said their goodbyes, then he and Grace went out to his SUV.

"He looks content," Grace said, rubbing her hands to warm them.

"He is. He and Jasmin had a rough road for a bit, but everything's smooth sailing now."

"Did you go to school with them?"

"I was a couple years ahead but knew them both. Small town and all."

Grace cocked her head. "Were you and Jasmin ever

an item?"

Cade laughed and started the truck. "No. She only had eyes for Luke. Then and now."

"Good." That pleased Grace.

"I did ask her out, though."

Her happy mood deflated like a hot air balloon with a broken burner. It must have shown on her face because Cade leaned over to kiss her. "Don't worry. She turned me down, and she's not 'the one who got away.' I'm happy for her and Luke. They're perfect for each other."

Somewhat mollified, Grace settled back in her seat as Cade pulled onto the road. "Where to next?" she asked.

"The beach?"

"It's pretty windy."

"We'll just drive along it, then. If the wind dies down, we'll get a walk in. If not,"—Cade glanced sideways at Grace—"we'll get our exercise in other ways."

Oooh, did she want those other ways. Every part of Grace heated up. "Then I hope we get gale force winds."

"Never wish for that. We had a pretty bad blow a few weeks ago. Caused quite a bit of damage."

Grace nodded. "I was on duty that night."

"So were my parents." Cade frowned. "I went to the clinic and helped out where I could. Mostly minor injuries, but a few that got sent on."

"To my hospital. I know. I treated them. It was a rough night."

As he navigated the dips in the hardpacked sand to get to the beach, Cade asked Grace to tell him more about why she'd chosen emergency medicine, beyond the polite response she'd given his parents when they'd dined together.

"To be honest, I think it had to do with not being a patient's doctor long term, at least initially. I love medicine, but I don't have the best bedside manner." *Dr. Ice.* Grace sighed.

When Cade pronounced—with a mischievous gleam in his eye—that she *had* seemed a bit uptight on the night they'd met, Grace punched his shoulder. "You were asking for it that night in the ER."

"I was," he agreed.

"Anyhow, I realized I had good instincts about triage and quick diagnoses. More often than not, my guesses were spot on. And I like being able to get patients past that first hump of an ER visit, to kick start their body to heal."

"Then hand them off to another doctor? I would think pride would make you want to see it through."

"Oh, trust me, I do see the more interesting cases through. I follow up with the doctor and I've consulted on cases."

He reached for her hand, settling it on his leg, a place she had become very comfortable with it being. "You did a great job following up on me. I've got no complaints."

"How is the ankle? Any issues since you ditched the boot and crutches?"

Cade shook his head. "Pain is gone, except for a twinge here and there. Feels strong, but I won't be skiing for a while."

"Good. Give it time to heal well."

She stared out at the ocean waves, mesmerized by their constant movement.

"Do you ski?" he asked.

"No. And probably never will. I see too many ski accidents."

"Hmmm. How about cross-country skiing? Interested in giving that a try?"

"I don't know. I'm not much for being out in the cold."

"We can pack a picnic, bota bag and all. Lay a blanket out in the snow. Fool around."

If they kept up the sexy talk, Grace was going to be flushed and warm all day. "When you put it that way, it does sound rather nice."

"Rather nice? That's all I get for a snow picnic and a hot make-out session?"

Grace chuckled. "You'd have to work pretty hard to make me forget the cold."

"I am up for that challenge, Dr. Grace."

She moved her hand higher up his thigh. "I do believe you are at that."

He waggled his eyebrows at her, making her laugh more.

"I don't think this wind is going to die down. How about we go find that spot I was telling you about and see about warming us both up."

Oh, yes, Grace wanted that very badly. She nodded, the lump in her throat keeping her from forming words.

Chapter Thirteen

Cade drove down the coast to the jetty, then up a hill to an overlook that gave them a panoramic view of the ocean.

"This is lovely, Cade."

He nodded, watching the dark blue waves froth white and hit the shore. The weather never mattered here. Oh, you learned to prepare for anything and layers were essential, but the ocean was majestic rain or shine and it never got old. "I come here sometimes to think or work out a problem. As a teen, I never really appreciated it. I was more interested in the female companion in the car."

"I bet your teen 'brain' was pretty focused."

The quip made him turn in his seat. Grace, enraptured with the view, was absolutely the most beautiful woman he'd ever seen. Her eyes shone green in the muted daylight and her blonde hair fell in waves down her back. He reached for a strand and wound it around his finger.

"I love your hair."

She faced him, her eyes alight with pleasure, her smile fading, replaced by something deeper, an ardor he matched. Her pink tongue slipped out, wetting lips he couldn't resist. With a gentle tug on the curl around his finger, Grace leaned in and their lips met. Heat shot through him and he became hard instantly. Her lips, soft and pliable, offered him everything. The world, the sunshine, the universe. Everything he'd ever wanted coalesced and Cade poured everything he had into showing her how much she affected him.

Grace pulled back, staring at him. "Something changed."

Breathing hard, Cade nodded. "I think I'm in love with you, Dr. Grace."

Her eyes widened and the heat that coursed through Cade's body turned to nervous sweat. Right up until her eyes softened and the edges of her lips quirked up.

"I'm getting there," she said.

Letting out the breath he didn't realize he'd held, Cade grinned. "I can live with that."

He kissed her again. Kissed her until his world stopped spinning, until he knew he never wanted to be anywhere else but by her side, until his soul breathed its own sigh of relief.

Cade Huntington had found his forever woman. He'd come home.

By the time they broke apart, the ocean was invisible behind a curtain of fog on the windshield. Sitting back in her seat, Grace's chest heaved. "You take my breath away, Cade."

"Darlin', I know the feeling." He flipped the key to start his truck and turned the defrost on high. "If we keep this up, I'm going to need a new defrost unit."

Grace chuckled. "We could just head to your place. Put ourselves out of this misery."

"Ahh, but it's such sweet misery," he said, reaching for her hand. "I'd like to prolong it." At least long enough to make sure there were no ghosts left in his closet. Cade swallowed a lump in his throat.

"Not too much longer, though, right? I feel like I'm about to burst at the seams."

"Not too much longer. Though, it's good to know this place still has its magic."

"I don't think it's this place, Cade. I think you're the magic."

"We're the magic." Cade gave her a peck, then put the car in drive. "What say we ditch the park walk due to the cold and head for the grocery store to grab a few things I need for dinner?"

"I think that bit of normalcy will do me good," Grace said.

God, he loved the blush that lingered on her cheeks. Cade silently vowed to do everything in his power to make sure Grace was so happy and satisfied that she'd never leave him.

Except they had one big hurdle to get over, and he wouldn't make love to Grace until they talked. She needed to know the last secret in his life. Cade could only pray she felt strongly enough about him to work past it. If he lost her—

Nope. Not going there. Not until he'd done whatever he could to convince her they were meant to be together.

"Are you all right?"

"Sure," he said, then cleared his throat. "Why?"

"You were frowning."

"Sorry. Just running over my grocery list in my head."

Grace nodded, seeming to accept his answer. Cade begged the fates that she'd accept what he had to tell her just as easily.

~~~

Shopping with Cade turned out to be fun. They were very compatible, discussing fruits, vegetables, and the best ingredients. Like mushrooms. Some people were very picky about them. It turned out that both she and Cade were that way, so no arguments there.

"You like asparagus, right?" He picked up a banded bunch.

"As long as they're not mushy."

"They won't be." He insisted on paying for the groceries. "My house, my meal, my cost."

Before long, they were on their way to his house. The grocery store had provided a very necessary respite for Grace. She needed a break from the strong emotions and the lust that coursed through her. There really was no other way to put it. She lusted after Cade. There was more to their relationship, though, and this was fresh territory for her. She'd never been so taken with someone. She needed Cade in her daily life. Not just to get by. Grace took care of herself quite well. She needed him to complete her. To be happy. How had that happened?

Her emotional state made tonight even more important. Were they compatible sexually like they were in every other aspect of their lives to date? God, she hoped so. She'd waited so long for this night. Well, maybe not specifically for Cade, but in some ways, her whole life had led up to this moment and Grace wanted to be everything to this wonderful man. To make sure he wouldn't leave her. Because, while she hadn't been quite ready to use the "L" word, she knew her world would be devastated if Cade wasn't in it. Whoa. Grace froze. Where had that come from? How had she let Cade in so deep? Old memories surfaced. Her mother setting her suitcase beside the door. "*I'll be back in a jif.*"

"Are you all right?"

Was she? Cade could hurt her. He could reopen the old wounds inflicted by her mother. How had she let things get so far so fast? Should they take a step back? No. Grace didn't want to. Not tonight. She'd worry about the rest tomorrow. She thrust the somber thoughts to the back of her mind and broke out in a genuine smile. She vowed to herself to live in the moment and let the night unfold as it would.

At Cade's, he set out the things he needed for dinner on the kitchen island while Grace put the cold stuff in the fridge. Just like couples who shopped together all the time. Grace liked this domesticity. It felt right. With vague surprise, she found the Christmas decorations didn't even bother her. Well, not much.

"Want some wine?"

She could use some relaxation. Was she enough for Cade? Would he want to stick around? No matter how hard she tried, old fears kept nudging her, not quite kept at bay. "Sure."

"The wine cooler is around the corner. Why don't you pick something out?"

Grace rounded the kitchen wall to find not one of those small, under-the-counter wine coolers, but a door into a separate room. Once inside, she realized it was climate controlled and filled with wine bottles from floor to ceiling. Mouth agape, she wandered around the small room, unable to even begin to pick out one wine from the vast selection.

"I forgot to tell you I have a pretty extensive wine collection," Cade said, joining her, his brow creased.

"Pretty extensive? There's a small fortune in wine here." How did he manage this on a cable repairman's salary?

Had his shrug seemed stilted? "I don't drink much, but I like a nice wine with dinner. It's my hobby, collecting wine." He picked up a bottle. "This should go well."

With his hand at the back of her waist, they returned to the kitchen. Grace sat while Cade opened the bottle.

"We'll just let this air a bit." He set it aside and

puttered at dinner fixings.

Tonight would be spinach salad, crab cakes, and the asparagus. The off-season crab had been expensive, but Cade had insisted. How did he afford all this? Something wasn't adding up. Right now, Grace got the distinct impression Cade didn't want to have a serious discussion about anything if the way he was puttering was any indication.

"The cable company must pay you pretty well," she said as he handed her a glass of wine. His hand shook. when he poured his own, his shoulders deflating.

"What's wrong, Cade? What aren't you telling me?" Worried now, Grace reached for Cade's white hand pressing into the counter.

He straightened, came around to sit next to her at the island, and turned her chair toward him. He placed his hands on her legs, head down for a moment. When he lifted it, her own worry was reflected in his eyes.

"You're scaring me," Grace said. "What's going on?"

"You've come to mean a lot to me."

"That goes both ways." She covered his tense hand with her own.

"I don't want to lose you."

If Grace weren't so freaked out right now, she'd laugh. Like he could do that. Lose her? She was in too deep. "What's so bad that you think you could lose me?"

"I have a secret."

Grace's spine stiffened. She picked up her glass and took a sip of wine, studying the misery on Cade's face. This must be big, which meant she wasn't going to like it. At all.

"And you don't like secrets. Or lies. I know that about you."

"Absolutely right," she said, suddenly unable to relax. Her muscles, stiff and sluggish, wouldn't respond.

Grace rubbed legs that had gone numb. "Just spit it out, Cade."

He took a gulp of his wine, something he never did. Cade savored wines. He collected them, for God's sake.

"You remember when you told me the story about your mother?"

"Like I could forget? I've never told anyone that story."

Cade cupped her cheek for a moment, then sat back. "That was a huge gift you handed me, trusting me with your past like that. Part of that story, at least what I heard between the lines, was that you don't want anything to do with the wealthy."

"You're right. Money was the reason my mother left us. We weren't good enough for her. I wasn't good enough."

"You are, though. That's the thing. You are an amazing woman and I'm quite sure you were an equally amazing kid."

Grace brushed the idea away with a wave of her hand. "What's this got to do with you?"

"I kind of have some."

"Some what? Money? You mean from your parents? You haven't once acted like someone who lived for money around me. So why is this an issue?"

"It's an issue because I wouldn't take money from my parents." He shook his head. "They offered but it came with too many strings attached. I— I made this money on my own."

"All right. So how much are we talking about? A nice retirement cache or more than that?"

"More. A lot more."

Grace's impatience was at its zenith. She was done coaxing the information out of him, so she slipped into Dr. Grace mode and glared at him.

"Wow," Cade said, taking a sip of wine this time,

not a gulp. "That doctor thing you do is downright scary."

Silent, Grace waited.

"All right. I'm a multi-millionaire. I make my money designing digital games. The cable thing is just a side gig because they couldn't find anyone to cover this area and I get all my connectivity free."

"You design games? You mean like *HALO* and *Roblox*?" She didn't understand. "How does that make you so much money?"

"Yes, like those games. In fact, I wish I'd thought of the *Roblox* idea. That team made much bigger bank than me. Gaming is a huge industry. Huge." He waved his hands in emphasis.

"So you design war games?"

"I've done a couple. Mostly, I do fantasy role-play games. Dragons and elves and such."

"And this has made you rich." Grace had trouble wrapping her head around how game design could be so lucrative. Another, darker emotion started to wrap itself around her heart, negative and withering. Cade was rich, and she wasn't. That kind of money could hurt and she didn't want to be around it. Ever. She'd never measure up.

"Yes," he said. "Designing games has made me a wealthy man. And all this time I've been afraid to tell you. I'd hoped that, once you got to know me, this little thing wouldn't matter." Cade flashed his award-winning smile, but it quickly disappeared. "You're angry."

Surprised that she was indeed angry, Grace pushed her wine glass away and stood up. "I'm angry." And scared. "And hurt. You lied to me."

"I omitted information. No, you're right. I lied. I wanted time, for you to get to know me and see past the money. I'm not your past, Grace. I'm your future. It may not have been right, but I can't take it back. I can only ask you to consider the reason behind the lie."

Lies are lies. The room closed in on Grace. The wine, the decorations, Cade's money. Everywhere she turned, Christmas laughed in her face. She needed out of there, time to think.

"A lie is a lie in my mind, and you know that or you wouldn't be so concerned right now." Grace kept her voice carefully modulated, like she'd learned in medical school. Don't show your fear. Keep it about the problem at hand. Except she could feel shreds being torn from her heart with every breath. He'd lied to her. And, with the kind of money he had, she couldn't be more than just a passing fancy. Cade Huntington could have any woman he wanted. Hell, he could buy them. Her breath hitched.

"I'm falling in love with you, Grace. I don't want to lose you." Cade reached for her, but she leaped up, backing into his second, smaller Christmas tree and almost knocking it over. She needed to get away from him. From here.

Pursing her lips to keep the emotions from bursting free, Grace walked to her purse and coat. "I need some time."

Cade tried to pull her into his arms but she stiffened, so he backed up a step. "Don't go, Grace. Please don't go. Let's talk this out. Get mad. Yell at me. Please. Let's work through it."

"I— I can't." Oh damn, her voice was shaking like she was eight years old again. She'd start crying in a minute. "Not right now. I— I need some time."

"All right." Cade hung his head. "I'll take you home."

She put a hand out. "No. I'll catch a rideshare. I just— I need to get out of here."

Grabbing her coat, she flew out the door just as the tears started to fall.

"Grace!" Cade called from behind her. But he didn't

follow her. If he had, she might have cold-cocked him, the way she was feeling. Grateful she was in comfortable shoes, Grace ran for several blocks before slowing down enough to pull her jacket on and look around at all the festive decorations. All around, Christmas crowded in on her. She wanted to rip it all to pieces.

Ruined again. What was it about holidays and lies? They swarmed her, whipping her emotions into a frenzy like water under a gale.

When she heard a car, Grace swiped at her tears, turning her face away. No need to let anyone in Willow Bay see her like this.

Whoever it was slowed down.

"Come on, Grace. Let me drive you home. Please?"

She couldn't get in the car with him.

"It's freezing and your phone fell out of your purse. Please." He kept even with her, driving slowly along the side of the road. "I promise, I won't say a word. I'll give you time to think. I just want to get you home safely."

Digging in her purse for her absent phone, Grace relented. The walk would be miles long and frigid in this dark, wet, cold town. Cade was right, damn it.

Without saying a word, she climbed in and belted up.

"Thank you."

Grace glared at him, no longer caring that he'd see the tear tracks on her face. His own eyes were filled with misery. She steeled her heart against it. He'd lied to her.

At her house, he pulled over and she opened the door. He stopped her with a hand on her arm but she'd be damned if she'd turn around. "I'm sorry, Grace. I'll do anything I can to make it up to you. Just tell me what to do."

"Leave me alone," she said, grinding the words out. She leaped from the truck, raced up her steps, then fumbled with the keys. When she finally got her door unlocked, she slammed it shut behind her and slumped to the floor, one part of her wishing he'd follow her and the other never wanting to see him again.

He'd lied to her, kept something from her that he knew would change her opinion of him. He had money. Lots of it, and she'd seen firsthand what money did to people. Her mother left her because of money. Back in Chicago, she'd seen so much corruption, so many people ruined by greed. Maybe Cade wasn't affected by the money yet, but he would be. Everyone succumbed to the lure of fortune sooner or later. If she stayed with him, her worst fear would be realized. She could not compete with that kind of wealth. Affluence would become more important to him than she was, and he'd tire of her—just like her mother had.

Grace put her face in her hands and screamed, trying to expel her fear. Better to be angry. Anger she could handle, but fear? Fear took control and left her with nothing but the shards of her ruined life.

Relationships sucked.

These thoughts ran through her mind as she sat there crying, wondering how she would ever pick up the pieces of her shattered heart and get on with her life.

Chapter Fourteen

Morning came and went before Cade managed to drag himself out of bed. After getting home, he'd corked the wine and dug for the Pendleton sipping whiskey tucked away in the cupboard over the fridge. He never drank except for wine. But last night, he'd finished a bottle of whiskey. And this morning he remembered why he didn't drink much.

In the kitchen, he downed two ibuprofen, filled a glass with ice water, and chugged it. Filling the glass again, he went to the sofa and sank onto it, unable to fathom how his life had turned to muck in so short a time.

He knew his part in it. He'd made a mess of things. A huge mess. By not coming clean right from the beginning, Cade may have lost the one person who gave life meaning. He ran his hands through his hair, then leaned his head back on the couch.

Cade wasn't going to apologize for who he was or what he did for a living. He'd found his niche and had carved out a lifestyle he enjoyed. Except he wanted Grace in that life. Now, she wanted nothing to do with him and it was all his fault. How could he make it up to her? Make her see how important she'd become to him.

His cell buzzed. Cade grabbed it, hoping it was Grace. It wasn't.

"Hi, Dad."

"Hello, son. Thought I'd check-in to see how you're doing."

Ridiculous. He'd spoken to his parents more in the last week than he had in the past year. "You mean you want to see if I'm alone or if I have company, right?"

His father chuckled. "I'm pretty transparent, aren't I?"

Hell, yeah, Cade thought but didn't answer.

"So, are you? Alone?"

"Yep."

His father breathed in before answering. "Well, that's disappointing."

"Yep."

Another couple of beats, then his father spoke again. "Are you all right, son?"

"Nope."

"I'm sorry."

"Because I'm not all right or because your clinic plans are slithering down the drain?"

"I won't apologize for wanting our clinic to thrive. Or for being disappointed you didn't choose to be a part of it. However, first and foremost is your well-being. Always."

That surprised Cade. He wasn't sure how to answer. "Thanks," he finally said.

"Anything I can do to help?"

"No. I have to figure this out for myself."

"You can do it, son. I have every faith in you. If you need any help, I'm here. Both your mother and I are here for you, despite what you might think."

His father rang off and Cade set the phone down, bemused. He'd never heard his father worried before, yet by the tone of his voice, he clearly was. Cade didn't think his parents worried about anything except the clinic. But this was a puzzle best left for another day. Cade had much more important things to think through.

Last night, Grace had reacted much worse than he'd expected. He found that hard to understand. His relationship with his parents might be strained, but he'd never experienced any soul-crushing moments in his childhood like Grace had. In his mind, he'd downplayed her devastation over her mother's abandonment. Like a complete ass, he figured he could sweep it under the rug with some Christmas decorations. He hadn't properly considered the effect that kind of trauma would have on anyone. Grace's mother had forged Grace's future when she deserted her, and she said she'd done it because she wanted a better life. How did that feel for Grace? Like she hadn't been enough of a reason for her mother to stick around? Who did that to their child?

An unfamiliar gratitude and love welled up in Cade. He'd had loving parents. Manipulative, sure. Focused on their plans for him. Definitely. But they'd always been there when he needed them. Linda Benson's one decision had made it all but impossible for Grace to trust anyone. If Grace couldn't get past this, there was no future for them. And he wanted that future so bad it scared him.

Still, Cade never shied away from a challenge. If he could help Grace deal with her past, maybe she could forgive him for withholding information.

But how? Her mother had left her hanging. Grace never got closure, never got to ask her mother why money was more important to her than her own daughter.

Grace needed closure. And Cade realized at that moment, even through the hangover haze, that he knew just how to bring that about.

He sat up suddenly, then sank back down holding

his head. Maybe he'd just lay here a while before doing anything. Take a nap and get rid of this horrendous headache. It galled him to have to wait, but he was in no condition to do anything. He closed his eyes, willing his body to rid itself of the toxins so he could put his plan into play and bring the love of his life back to him.

~~~

She'd about had it with downtime. Her day off gave Grace time to think, and think, and think. She'd called the hospital, hoping she could go into work. They'd emphatically denied her request. Something about regulations and how she'd worked too many hours this pay period already. Like she could rest. All she could do was think about Cade and last night.

God, she missed him. She missed talking to him, laughing with him, kissing him. What she didn't miss was the lie between them. She'd trusted him with her deepest secret and, in return, he'd withheld a basic fact about his life? Why didn't he trust her with this one, big, huge, relationship-changing thing? All his silence did was bolster her feeling that the money was important to him. Some part of her argued that he'd never shown one bit of interest in money, but anger overrode everything. Anger and hurt.

Grace had spent the entire day trying to find a way past it, to no avail. Deep down, she knew it wasn't the lie that bothered her so much as her past screaming into the present. She'd been found lacking before. She'd be found lacking again. Maybe it was best to be the one to end things. Leave before she got left.

Shutting the book she'd been trying to read for the past hour, she got up and went to the window to look out at the gray drizzle. Even the weather seemed out of sorts. Certainly not good for walking. Not good for hair either. She'd never dealt with friz until she'd moved to the beach. Smoothing her hair, she wished Cade's hands were there. In her hair, on her neck, her body.

Damn. Grace needed to get out of this house. Sitting by herself at some restaurant didn't sound like much fun, but there wasn't anywhere else she could go and she didn't feel like cooking dinner. Cade had mentioned a pizza place in town, so she grabbed her coat and purse, slipped on her shoes, and headed out the door without thinking twice. If she spent one more hour in the house, imagining Cade cooking in her kitchen, lying in her bed, she was going to scream.

A few minutes later, Grace walked into Square Peg. The décor provided an immediate distraction. The walls—full of memorabilia, farm instruments, old movie posters, and license plates—fascinated her. She strode around a wall to get a better look at some of the stuff, right into the arms of a life-sized, carved bear with an orange Easter peanut in its hand.

"Oh!" She jumped back just as a man walked by.

"Sorry," Grace said.

"No worries. Harry there gets to everybody on their first visit." He smiled, his blue eyes crinkling at the edges.

"He's, umm, unusual."

"Yes, but people remember us because of him."

"And the wall decorations, I'd imagine."

"And the pizza."

"That's what brought me in."

"Great. Grab a seat and I'll get you a menu."

Grace sat in a booth and glanced out the window at the day's ever-present drizzle. The gray matched her emotional state. Why had she moved to the Washington coast? She should have picked California or Florida. Except California had too many people and Florida was too humid.

"Here you go," the man said, setting a glass of water and a menu down.

"Thanks." Grace looked at him. He was about her

age, which seemed unusual for someone working in a pizza joint. "Do you own this place?"

"Yes. Along with my wife, who's upstairs resting feet worn out by this place and our soon-to-be-born baby." He grinned from ear to ear, obviously proud. "I'm Paul Gibson."

"Hi, Paul. I'm Grace Benson. Dr. Benson."

"Obstetrical?" he said, with obvious hope in his voice.

She shook her head. "Emergency room. Grays Harbor General"

"Oh. We go there for our prenatal care. I was just hoping maybe someone would set up an OB office here in town."

"Doesn't the clinic provide those services?" Cade's parents had mentioned they were pretty much full-service general practitioners along with the urgent care.

"Yes, but Bernie wanted an OB."

Grace nodded. A lot of people felt that way. And truly, it was the safest way to go. "I can understand that."

"Well, I'll give you a chance to look at the menu."

"Thanks, but I don't need to. I'll have your Caesar salad and a veggie pizza, personal size."

"Great. I'll get that going. Anything else to drink?"

"No, thank you. Water is fine."

"All right. Won't take long. The dinner rush hasn't started yet, as you can probably tell by the empty tables."

"Mind if I wander around, check out the walls?"

"Help yourself." He disappeared into the kitchen and Grace got up to browse the wall art, smiling when she heard Paul humming lullabies in the kitchen. Oh, yes, he was excited for this baby.

Her salad arrived just as she sat back down. Grace dove into it, surprised to find herself hungry. Thinking back, she realized this was the first thing she'd eaten that day. She was never this bad about food, not even at work.

Food equaled energy, which got her through her shifts.

When Paul set her pizza down, Grace took a big whiff. "Smells great."

"Thank you."

"I've been wanting to come here ever since Cade mentioned it." Damn, why had she mentioned Cade? And why did uttering his name stab at her heart?

"Cade Huntington?"

"Yes. He's, ummm, been showing me around." Not an outright lie, but not the whole truth either.

Paul grinned. "No one better to teach you about Willow Bay."

"He's... been great." She did not want to talk about Cade. At all.

"If you need a character reference, you'll get one from me and Bernie," Paul said, watching her closely. "He's a good friend and a stand-up guy."

Oh, Lord, this was going from bad to worse. Willow Bay, backing up one of its own. Fighting the tears forming behind her eyes, Grace took refuge in the only thing she could—her doctor attitude. "Thank you for that recommendation."

"Yes, well, I've overstayed my welcome," Paul said, smiling. "I'll leave you to your pizza."

Now she was alienating Cade's friends. "I'm sorry, Paul." She meant it. "I'm just— not sure about Cade. That's no reason to take it out on you."

Paul gave a quick nod of acceptance. "Want to talk about it?"

Definitely not. "No. I just need to think."

"Well, if you ever want to talk, Bernie and I both have awesome listening ears."

"Thanks." Grace's smile was genuine. She liked Paul and she'd bet anything she'd like his wife, too.

"I'll let you eat now." Paul moved back behind the counter just as a family of four entered.

Grace watched him seat what appeared to be a father, mother, an adorable little girl, and a baby still in the carrier. A strong longing surprised Grace. She'd never wanted children. The worry, always at the back of her mind, that she would flub raising children as badly as her mother had, kept her from considering the possibility. Old enough to know that she was not her mother, Grace still hesitated. But right now, at this moment, she regretted that choice when a powerful yearning stole her breath away.

She thought of Cade. What would a child of theirs look like? Would it inherit her bent toward medicine? His wonderful laugh that went all the way to his dark eyes?

A warm glow filled her, adding to the craving. Grace shook her head vehemently, chomping down on a piece of pizza. She missed Cade, and that made her angry with herself. What was she supposed to do, just forgive him? She'd bared her soul about her mother. Knowing what she'd told him, he still withheld information he had to know would trigger her.

How could she shove it all aside? If she didn't, though, she'd lose Cade. And that wounded her more than anything. Grace had come to love having Cade in her life. Did she love *him*? She loved being with him, loved kissing him, loved everything about him. She missed his touch, his silly grin, his goofy lust look.

Was that love? Grace didn't know. She pushed the pizza away, no longer hungry. Signaling for Paul, she asked for a box and was soon on her way back to her empty house. She settled back in her chair and picked up her book, but couldn't focus.

Instead of reading, Grace stared out the window at the dark night, trying to define love and what it meant to feel that way. And how to reconcile the Cade she knew with this new man who decided, without asking her, what was best for her by omitting vital information about himself that he knew would hurt her. No one did that. Not to Grace Benson, damn it.

No easy answers came to her.

Chapter Fifteen

Two days before Christmas. Cade sat in the break room of Grays Harbor General Hospital, more nervous than he'd ever been before. He was about to take the biggest gamble of his life. If this worked, Grace could finally move beyond her past and find happiness. Cade prayed that happiness would include him, but this was more about her. She needed to get beyond the pain of her mother's desertion.

The woman sitting across from him looked as nervous as he felt. Her eyes—the same dark hazel as Grace's—shifted from his face to the table and she wrung her hands over and over. "Are you sure it's a good idea to do this here?"

"I think it's the best place. She can't create a scene. She'll have to hear you out."

"I don't like putting her on the spot like this. We should have called first." The woman stood up as the door to the lounge opened and Grace Benson walked in.

"Cade? What's wrong? Why are you here?" she asked, her gaze turning to finally take in the woman standing near him.

Grace froze, and Cade held his breath. She looked at the woman, her stare growing colder with each passing second. She turned to Cade, her face a hard mask.

"What is she doing here?" Grace's monotone voice scared the hell out of Cade. Maybe he'd made the wrong choice.

"I found your mother, and you two need to talk," he said, his own voice a pittance of its normal timbre.

"I won't speak with her."

"Grace," the woman said.

"No." Grace slashed her hand through the air. "I don't want to hear a word you have to say." She whirled on Cade. "And you. After that Christmas decoration debacle, you should know better than to throw something like this at me. How dare you interfere in my life? You don't get to make choices for me. We're done."

Oh, shit. She was really and truly pissed. Cade knew he only had seconds to repair this before she walked out of his life. And God, he just couldn't let that happen. He couldn't lose her. Not now. Not ever.

"Please don't leave."

She stopped mid-stride, shaking her head, not turning around. "How could you?"

"I did it for you." He gripped her shoulders with gentle care. "To help you come to terms with your past."

"Get your hands off me," she said in full on doctor voice. When he did so with haste, Grace turned slowly around. "Let me make this perfectly clear. This,"—she waved toward where her mother stood—"was not your choice to make. It was mine and I made the decision long ago that I would have *nothing* to do with her. You ripped that choice from my heart and stomped on it."

"I know I've hurt you," her mother said. "Please give me a chance to explain."

Cade could hear the tears in the woman's voice, but he didn't turn around. He stayed focused on Grace. Reaching for her hand, he flinched when she yanked it away.

The lounge door opened. "Emergency, doctor. We need you now."

With a nod, Grace whipped around. Before she got through the door she looked back at Cade, her face a mask of non-emotion. "Be gone when I get back." She glanced at her mother. "You, too."

~~~

Grace shook with anger. How could he have done that?

"Doctor, I need your attention," Stan the charge nurse said.

"Sorry." Grace took a deep breath. "What's the situation?"

"Heart attack. Serious. He'll be here in moments. They've been doing CPR for about fifteen minutes. Some doctor from Willow Bay."

Stan gave her the clipboard and she glanced at the name. Huntington. Cade's father. Her heart raced as the bay doors opened and a stretcher was brought in. A paramedic crouched on top of the patient doing compressions.

"Tell the man in the lounge to wait for me."

"What? Looked like you were having issues."

"Doesn't matter. This is his father. Don't tell him. I'll talk to him as soon as I'm able."

"Done," Stan said as Grace flew into the room right behind the stretcher, trying to think through the chaos all around her and the turmoil in her heart and head. But she'd always been able to compartmentalize. Her skills kicked in and Dr. Grace Benson started giving orders. Twenty minutes later, Cade's father was still alive and stable, for the moment. They'd had to shock him three more times before his heart started beating on its own again.

Stan stayed with Mr. Huntington as Grace stepped out to go talk to Cade. As she walked down the hall, her legs failed her and she leaned against the wall, digging for some, any, strength. She'd almost lost Cade's father. The adrenaline ebbed from her body and she sank to the floor, tears filling her eyes. Tears of relief, tears of disappearing anger, tears of fear for Lawrence Huntington. He wasn't out of the woods yet.

And now she had to tell Cade. And face her own mother again. Grace stood, grateful no one had seen her fade like that. Straightening her clothes, she wiped the tears from her face and strode into the break room.

Cade's back was to the door. He sat talking to her mother, whose face was ravaged by tears. Why? Grace was the wronged party. Why would her mother be crying?

No. That woman wasn't why she was here. "Cade?"

He turned and rushed to her side. "You've been crying. What's wrong?"

"Can I talk to you outside?"

"Sure, honey. Sure. Anything you want."

In the hall, she stuck her sweaty hands in her pockets. "Your father is okay at the moment, but he's had a heart attack."

"I'm sorry. I never meant— Wait, what?"

The look of confusion on Cade's face verified he hadn't moved past their disagreement. But that was for another time.

"Your father is here, in our ER. He had a massive heart attack."

"Dad? What? How?"

At that moment, Cade's mother flew through the emergency room doors, her cell phone in her hand. "Where is he? Where's my husband?"

"Mom?"

Grace could see Cade's confusion and distress deepening. "Cade, you're Dad's a patient here," she said. "He had a heart attack."

"I was just calling you," his mother said.

"Where is he?" Cade and his mom spoke at the same time.

"Before I take you to him, let me catch you up. Why don't we step in here where it's quieter?"

"No. I want to see my husband."

"Dr. Huntington, I understand that." Grace put a hand on the woman's arm. "But if you go in there all upset, the only thing you will accomplish is to worry an already very sick man." Grace looked at Cade with a silent plea.

"Come on, Mom. Let's hear what Grace has to say. She's the doctor here." Cade led his mom back to the lounge where, only minutes ago, Grace had come undone. She followed them to find her mother still sitting there. Steeling herself, Grace turned to Cade and his mother. "Are you all right discussing this in front of her?" She indicated her own mother.

"Yes."

"I don't care. How is my husband?"

"He's had a massive myocardial infarction," Grace said. "Thank goodness he coded at the clinic because people knew what to do."

Michelle Huntington sank into a chair, wringing her hands. "I only left for half an hour to grab us all some lunch."

Grace squatted down and placed her hands on Michelle's. "I'm quite sure your husband is alive because of how fast the people at your clinic acted. Not that this isn't serious." She glanced up at Cade.

"Tell us everything," he said.

"They were still doing compressions when they brought your husband in. They shocked him at the clinic, twice in the ambulance, and three times here, along with meds. It was touch and go, but we got him back." She squeezed Michelle's hand. "We got him back. He's alive."

"It's serious, though." Grace stood. "If he's stable for another hour, we'll take him for testing to define what damage has been done."

Cade's mother stood as well, wiping at her eyes and nodding, much more in control of herself. "In these cases, the damage can be extensive."

"Yes. He'll have a long road to recovery." His days of working as a doctor would probably end as well, but better to address that when they knew more. "Once testing is done, he'll go to the coronary care unit." Hopefully, not the ICU.

"All right. I understand. And I've calmed down. Can I see him now?"

Grace smiled. "Follow me." She led them out the door and down the hall. Cade's mother went in, but Grace stopped Cade. He looked ravaged. "You can't go in there looking like the world is ending."

"I know." Cade leaned against the wall. "But I have to see him. I need to see him."

"Right now, it's about what he needs."

Cade scrubbed his face with both hands. "He's always been the strong one. I— I don't know how to handle this."

"One day at a time." She took both his hands in hers. "One hour at a time. He's alive. Focus on that."

He nodded, holding her gaze like a starved man. "Thank you, Grace. If you hadn't been here… "

"Someone else equally capable would have been."

When he cupped her cheek, Grace leaned into it.

"Still, I feel better that it was you."

"Thank you," she whispered. "Now go see your father."

Cade glanced back down the hall. "I forgot. Your mother."

Grace pursed her lips. "I'll get her an Uber back to

wherever she's staying."

"Thank you, Grace. I'm— I'm sorry. For everything."

"I know," she said. "Now go."

She watched him walk into the treatment room and heard his voice shake with emotion.

"Way to grab all the attention, Dad."

With a fleeting smile, Grace went to the nurse's station and grabbed Lawrence Huntington's chart, updating the orders.

"I've notified CCU. They've got a bed ready and will take him directly from radiology. And the cardiologist will be here within the next few minutes," Stan said.

"Thanks." She closed the chart and turned around to look at the door to the lounge. This was not something she wanted to do. At all. She needed to get past it so she could focus on more important things. "I'll be in the break room. Grab me if anything changes."

"Will do."

Grace dragged leaden feet to the door. Taking a long breath to calm her surprisingly rattled nerves she pushed it open. Her mother stood and waited for Grace to speak.

Her doctor's eye took over. The woman had aged a lot. She had deep lines in her forehead and around her mouth, indicating she hadn't had the best life. She was only, what, forty-nine? If she'd hooked up with money, Grace would have expected her to use it to maintain a youthful appearance. There must be more to Linda Benson—if that was still her name—than the history Grace knew. She mentally shook herself, not wanting to feel any sympathy for the person she used to call mother. It was time to be done with this.

"Where are you staying?" Grace asked.

"At the Motel 6."

She'd expected to hear Pacific Lodge, the most upscale place in town. Why was she at the motel? No.

Grace refused to ask. "You heard what's going on with Cade's father, right?"

Her mother nodded. "Grace— "

Grace held up a hand. "This isn't the time or place. I'll get an Uber to take you back. I don't think Cade will want to leave."

"I can find my way back. I'll walk."

"No need." Grace eyed her mother's outfit. Jeans, long-sleeved shirt and a hoodie, but no hat. No purse. And shoes that looked pretty old and worn. "I'm getting you an Uber. Please don't argue. Follow me."

Her mother followed and, once in the right spot, Grace ordered the Uber. She decided to stay and make sure her mother got in. Why she cared, she had no idea.

"I'm sorry, Grace."

Deep in thought, Grace didn't think she heard her mother right. "What?"

"I'm sorry. For everything. That's all I came to say. I get that you don't want anything to do with me. I accept that."

Grace opened her mouth, speechless. Did her mother think she could wipe out the memory, the pain, with an apology? It would take a lot more than that. Grace didn't have the words to express her anger, her conflicted emotions. Thankfully, the Uber pulled up. Grace opened the back door without saying a word. Her mother—her eyes full of misery Grace didn't want to acknowledge—got in.

"I love you, Gracie. Always have. Always will." She shut the door and the Uber pulled away.

For a few seconds, Grace stood there shaking. Tears fell unchecked as twenty years of hurt tore at her insides, gutting her. She ran back into the ER, past a surprised Stan at the station, straight to the women's room and into the disabled stall, crouching down against the wall as she cried, unable to stop herself. Unable to prevent the memories from playing over and over in her mind.

Unable to accept what she'd just witnessed—that her mother was a real person with real problems of her own.

~~~

Cade sat at his dad's bedside, holding his mother's hand and trying to make sense of the day's events. His father slept, thanks to the meds. And the steady beep, beep, beep of the monitor reassured Cade that his heart, for the moment, had good rhythm.

Lawrence Huntington had always been the rock of Cade's family, the strong one. Sometimes too strong and too opinionated. But Cade had always known his father loved him and that he'd be there for him no matter what. Now, he looked so small, laying on the gurney with wires and tubes everywhere. God, how had this happened?

Sure, his dad wasn't much into exercise. There wasn't time with all his hours at the clinic. But he ate well. The man was a stickler for good nutrition and he hardly had any stomach paunch. What had caused this? Was it hereditary? Or stress-related? He knew his dad worked at the clinic from open to close. Sometimes later. Was that why this had happened? Guilt overrode worry. Could Cade have kept this from happening by going to med school and helping out? God, was this his fault? Deep down, Cade knew these thoughts were ridiculous, but that didn't stop the regret from taking hold.

"We have to believe he'll come through this," his mother whispered, squeezing Cade's hand.

"He will. He has to," Cade answered, trying to believe the pale face laying there could rebound.

Stan and an orderly came in. "We're going to take him for an ECG now," Stan said, bustling around and disconnecting tubes and wires. The orderly rehung the IV bags on a pole he attached to the gurney.

"ECG?" Cade said.

"Echocardiogram," his mother answered. "An ultrasound to check how much damage has been done."

"That's right." Stan nodded. "The cardiologist will meet him there. Afterward, he'll go straight to CCU. Room two. The specialist won't come talk with you until the tests are completed, so this would be a good time for you to get something to eat. The cafeteria food's pretty good. I can show you how to get there."

"Can we sit here for a few minutes?" Cade's mother said. "We're still getting our wits about us."

"Sure. Five or ten minutes will be fine unless the open rooms fill up. I'll let you know if that happens."

They nodded their thanks as the orderly wheeled Cade's father out of the trauma room. Cade sat back down, staring at the empty space, now nothing but a couple of dropped bandages and garbage from electrodes. A mostly empty hole, just like Cade's heart.

"I'd better call the clinic," his mother said.

"Want me to?"

"No." She patted Cade's hand. "I'm in better shape now. I'll update them."

"Okay. I'll ask the nurse where the cafeteria and CCU are." Cade stood to leave but turned back. "Has he been working too hard at the clinic?"

His mother sighed. "We both probably have. But nothing indicated he wasn't well. Sometimes, these things happen out of nowhere."

"When things calm down, I'd like to talk about the clinic and its future."

"Yes, I think we need to do that. When we know better what's going on with your father."

"Sounds good." Cade walked down the hall and found Stan standing in front of the ladies' room, looking decidedly worried.

"Everything okay?" Cade asked.

"I'm not sure. Our only physician ran in here about

ten minutes ago and hasn't come out yet." He pointed at the door. "She looked pretty upset."

Just like that, Cade's heart was right back in his throat. "What happened?"

"I have no idea. She led the woman you came in with outside and raced past several minutes later. Looked like she was crying."

Acting on instinct, Cade opened the door. Short, quick whimpers came from the biggest stall. He nudged its door. Locked.

"Grace?"

"Go away."

"Grace, you're crying. Let me in."

"No."

"I'll crawl underneath if I have to. Please. Let me in."

"Please, Cade, just leave me alone. I'm a mess."

"And I want to help." He stayed put, aware she could see his feet beneath the short door. After several beats, he heard her move and raised his eyes to the ceiling with a silent thank you when she unlatched the door.

Pulling her into his arms, Cade didn't ask, didn't talk. He just held her and let her cry. God, had he done this? Had bringing Grace's mother here been this traumatic for her? Of course, it had. And he'd done it at her place of work. He was an idiot. Once again, without thinking, he'd put Grace in an emotional situation without giving her a choice in the matter. On the brink of Christmas, when her vulnerability was heightened.

"I'm sorry, Grace. I never should have done this the way I did. I'm so sorry your mother affected you this way. God, I never wanted to upset you. To make you cry. I only wanted to help. To make it easier for us to be together." Recognition hit him like an electrical shock. He'd done this as much, or more, for himself as he had for Grace. He was just about the most selfish bastard he'd ever known.

He kept murmuring to her as she cried. Damn, he'd never had a woman cry in his arms this hard for this long. Cade felt like a world-class heel.

It took a while, but Grace's tears ebbed. When she stepped back, her light makeup had run down her cheeks. Cade grabbed a towel from the dispenser and wet it, planning to wipe her tears away. She took the towel from him and went to the sink counter. She splashed her face and cleaned up. Turning back to Cade, she leaned against the counter as far away from him as she could be.

"Thank you for holding me. Apparently, I needed a good cry."

Cade, wishing she was back in his arms, didn't like the finality in her low, monotone voice.

"Are you all right?"

"No. But I will be."

"Good." He took a step toward her, stopping when she held up her hand.

"I can appreciate what you were trying to do by finding my mother, Cade. But I don't condone it. You made a rash decision—again—when you knew I wanted nothing to do with her.

"But I— "

"No. I heard you apologize while I was broken and crying. I do not accept it. I can't be with someone who has no regard for my choices or my wishes. You— " Her voice broke. "I actually thought you might be the one. I fell for you, Cade. Big time. Actually thought about the "L" word. But for you to do this, after the debacle with the decorations... I thought you'd learned—I have buttons that should not be pushed."

"I should have learned. I— "

"I don't want to hear it. Not anymore." She sniffed, took a last look in the mirror, then looked him square in the face with eyes more dead than alive. "We're done.

Your father's care has been transferred so there's no longer a reason for you to be in the ER. I'd like you to leave. And don't contact me again, please. Honor my wish this once, Cade. I can't take any more." She slipped out without saying another word.

He started to follow her, then stopped. Right now, nothing he could say would make a difference. Dr. Grace was in charge. She had a right to be pissed. Cade had screwed up royally and all he could do now was pray that she would come around. That the depth of her feeling for him would bring her back. Because Cade knew now that he loved Grace. Irrevocably, totally, permanently, and all the other adverbs he couldn't think of right at this moment.

With his heart weighing like a boulder in his chest, Cade checked the lounge and found Grace's mother gone. He joined his own mother and they headed for the cafeteria. As Cade walked out of the emergency room where he'd fallen in love for the first time ever, he hoped with everything he had that he hadn't screwed up this relationship for forever, that they could get past this. Please.

Chapter Sixteen

Grace walked out to her car like a zombie, unlocking the door, climbing in, and turning on the engine to warm the car up without thought. So much drama today. She didn't like drama. She didn't *do* drama. So why had today erupted into a volcano of emotional crises?

Because she'd let her heart guide her. Grace gripped the steering wheel. She'd learned this lesson a long time ago. Never lead with your heart because it will only get broken. She pressed a fist to her chest, pushing against the pain. Damn it. This didn't happen to her. She didn't hand her heartstrings to anyone because when the yank happened—and it always did—she paid too high a price.

This time, with Cade, was the worst ever. Cade, with his smile that melted ice queens, with his heart that just wanted to fix things for everyone, with his stubborn streak and inability to listen to what she wanted or needed. Grace shook her head. She put the car in drive and pulled out onto the rainy road for the dark, wet, lonely trip home.

Cade had screwed up. He never should have searched for her mother. That wasn't his call to make, and Grace had made the only choice she could. So why did she feel she'd let him down? No. Grace refused to go there. She'd made the right decision for herself, for her life. Her mother had deserted her years ago and no one, especially Cade, could change that.

Rain pelted the windshield. Grace focused on the road. Halfway home, she realized didn't remember any part of the drive. It was scary. Wind whipped the rain sidewise, pulling the car as she gripped the wheel. In the dark and rain, it was hard to see the road. Grace slowed and focused on the lane divider. It took her longer than any other trip home, but she made it. Driving past the holiday lights, vivid even in the rain, hadn't been easy. She pulled up in front of her house, clenching and unclenching her hands as she took some deep breaths and stared out at the pounding rain. Just like her mood. And no way to get inside without a soaking, either.

Nothing to do but go for it, so Grace snugged her day bag to her side and opened the car door, jumping out as she hit the lock button. Racing up to her porch, she almost missed the familiar SUV as it drove by.

Cade. Had he wanted to talk to her? Or was he just making sure she got home safe? This wasn't exactly what she'd meant when she told him not to contact her again. Grace couldn't decide if she was angry or touched. Touched in the head, more likely. She let herself in, locked the door, and walked to her kitchen island. Unpacking her day bag comforted her. Routine. That's what she needed. Her old routine.

Grace made herself some dinner, glancing up every time a pair of headlights passed out front. One part of her wanted Cade to knock on her door, but the other knew they just couldn't be. She shut all her blinds, trying to close the outside world away, at least for the evening.

Settled on her couch with a dollop of Irish cream in her coffee, Grace clicked through channels, unable to find anything that wasn't Christmas-related. She turned the television off. Her phone rang and her heart sped up until she saw it wasn't Cade.

"Hi, Dad."

"Hey, kiddo. Thought I'd check-in and see how you were doing. Are you at home?"

Fishing much? "Yes. I'm home. Alone. How are you?"

"Good. Just sitting here with Jackie, thinking about you."

Checking to make sure she was safe, just like Cade, because it was almost Christmas Eve and he knew how it affected her. Damn it. Stop thinking about Cade.

"How's life for you, Dad?"

"It's good. Really good, in fact. I, um, well, Jackie and I have decided to move in together."

Grace sat up, almost spilling her coffee and knocking the coffee table hard with her knee. "Ouch."

"You all right?" her Dad asked.

"Yes, I just hit the coffee table. I'm fine."

"So, what do you think, kiddo? Can you deal with your old man living in sin with a lady he's over the top in love with?"

She paused. It had always been just the two of them. Her and her dad. Now this woman she'd never met had slipped past his defenses and into his heart. Up until now, he'd been as dead to love as she'd been. Jackie had changed that for him, just as Cade had for her. Did Grace have the right to dampen her father's happiness just because her own love life had gone sour? No. She wouldn't do that. She couldn't.

"I'm happy for you, Dad."

"Thank you. Jackie is wonderful and I want you two to meet. Soon. You'll like her, Gracie. I know you will. She's amazing."

Grace smiled, though it was bittersweet. At least love had worked out for someone. "You sound really happy."

"I am. Though, that was a pretty pregnant pause before you responded. Something going on there?"

"Nothing I can't handle."

The silence on the other end of the line meant her father wasn't about to accept that answer from her. Grace didn't want to hash everything out. Didn't want to even talk about it right now, but she knew her father. He wouldn't let it go. If she didn't tell him tonight, he'd call tomorrow and every day after until he wore her down.

"I saw my mother today."

The pause on the other end of the line lengthened. Grace heard a feminine "what," then a mumbled, "She saw Linda."

"Dad?"

"I'm here. I was just filling Jackie in. This wasn't what I expected to hear. What— How did this come about?"

"The man I was seeing found her in his quest to make me like Christmas again."

"Ah, and that made you angry."

"Furious." Even now, the anger could build up. Overshadowed by her aching heart, but there nonetheless.

"How was it? Seeing your mother? Talking to her."

"I didn't talk to her. He— he brought her to the ER. To my work, Dad."

Her father sighed. "Your man has some learning to do."

"He's not my man. Not anymore. And I didn't talk to mom. I had an emergency to take care of, then I put her in an Uber back to her motel."

"Gracie, I think it might be time to let this all go."

"No, Dad. You don't get to say that to me. I'm glad you've found someone and you're happy. But that's not for everyone. Not for me. I will never forgive my mother.

I can't. And I can't forgive Cade for forcing me to try. I'm just done. With all of it."

"I get that. If I know you at all, I know you won't be able to let all this go so easily. But think about it, Grace. Anger takes so much energy. Maybe it's time to let it rest. I have, and I can't describe how much better I feel because of it. How much better my life is, day in and day out."

"Your life. Not mine."

"True. But you could have the same happiness. The love."

"I have love. Yours. I don't need anything else."

"Well, just think on it. And let's find a way to get together in person. Soon."

"I'll see if I can take some vacation next month and fly out for a visit. It will be quick, but I'd like to see you. And meet Jackie."

After the call ended, Grace picked up her now cold coffee. The day's events whirled around in her head. Her father, obviously happy, thought she should let go of twenty years of anger and a life where she'd found contentment. For what? To be happier?

Grace was happy. She had a home she loved. Granted, she hadn't been able to make the changes she wanted yet, but that would come with time.

Her job was fulfilling. Except, not so much lately. She'd become frustrated with unyielding work hours and mandatory overtime, even with her recent surprise days off. Had they known she was stressed out? What she'd thought would be small-town emergencies like tonsilitis, ankle sprains, and heart attacks had turned out to be many of the same problems. Less knifings, more overdoses. Less gunshot wounds, more drownings. So why had she gone into emergency work? Grace knew the answer, though it bothered her to recognize it. She didn't have to get involved with her patients in her line of work.

She could see them, treat them, then pass them off to their regular physicians.

She didn't have to care.

Had she designed her entire life around that premise? Staring into the mocha-colored coffee, she knew the truth. Yes, that's exactly what she'd done. She'd let the fear of being rejected again determine her choices. Grace got up and dumped her coffee in the sink. Holding onto the counter's edge, she stared at the tiled wall in front of her. To push the thoughts out of her mind, she focused on the old-style square tiles with flowers on every fourth tile, one of the things she wanted to modernize. Turning around, she leaned against the counter and went over her list. She'd keep all the dark molding around doors and entries, keep the curved arch between the kitchen and the dining/living room, but widen it.

Marrying the old with the new. That's what she wanted to do with this house. And that's probably what she should do with her life. Except it meant dealing with twenty-year-old pain. Talking to her mother. Grace wasn't sure she could do it. What reason could a woman have for deserting her child? Nothing that could compare to the pain Grace had gone through for twenty years.

Her mother had looked whole, not broken. But not happy either, with deep lines in a face full of sorrow and pain. Now that she'd seen her, could she ignore her?

Grace's natural desire to solve puzzles helped her in her chosen field. Now, she couldn't quite let go of the look on her mother's face. She gripped the counter, thinking about it all until her head ached. She realized she needed answers to this puzzle. It was time to understand.

Grabbing her phone, she searched for the motel where her mother had taken the Uber. Before she could change her mind, she called.

~~~

The next morning, the roads were unusually barren. It took a moment for Grace to remember today was Christmas Eve. Most of Willow Bay was probably in Olympia for last-minute shopping, or home wrapping gifts. All the things she'd shied away from for so many years. This had always been just another day to her. Now, she wished Cade were here. Especially with what she was about to do. She reached for the heater, though her shaking hands had nothing to do with being chilled. Her stomach lurched, tossing bile into her throat. Grace pulled over to the side of the road, afraid she would be sick to her stomach.

She shouldn't have called her mother. She could still turn around, just disappear like Linda Benson had. Her mind and heart ached for the eight-year-old in her, wanting a mother's love. The adult in her knew that was impossible. But she owed herself some answers, didn't she? After taking a few deep breaths, Grace pulled back out onto the road.

Her mother stood outside under the portico of the motel, waiting. Grace waved her over. She climbed into the SUV.

"I thought we'd go back to my house to talk," Grace said. "Quieter. Fewer ears."

"Makes sense." She nodded. "Thank you, Grace, for seeing me. I know this is a lot to ask."

Grace bit her lip to keep her comments back. This wasn't the time for anger, but for listening. Maybe for understanding. Only time would tell.

The silent, tense ride back to Grace's house about unraveled her last nerve. Once parked, she led the way up the stairs and unlocked the door, letting her mother enter first.

Linda Benson looked around the living room. Grace tried to see it from her eyes. New paint, old wood. New furniture, old floors.

"This looks homey," Linda said.

"Thank you." Grace took Linda's coat and hung it on the hall tree with her own. Luna wandered over and rubbed up against Linda. *Traitor.*

"The place looks like you."

"How do you know?" Okay, that was catty, and Grace hung her head for a moment, regretting her words. "I'm sorry. This isn't meant to be a spiteful day."

Her mother reached for her arm, then pulled back as if thinking better of it. "You have every right."

"Can I get you something to drink?" Was her mother an alcoholic? Was that why she'd left? Grace's father had never said anything, but it was in the realm of possibility. Plus, it would explain her haggard appearance and the deep lines on her face. "I have coffee, juice, water. Nothing alcoholic."

"I don't' do alcohol," Linda said. "Not for years. Coffee would be nice."

Maybe she's a recovering alcoholic? Grace couldn't help trying to read between the lines and solve this puzzle before Linda gave her the key.

"Cream? Sugar?"

"Creamer only. If you have something flavored?"

"Vanilla."

"Perfect."

While Grace busied herself in the kitchen, Linda picked up Luna and walked around the house, stopping to look at the pictures on Grace's mantle and absently petting the cat. The pictures were all of her father and her. Grace joined Linda, setting a tray on the coffee table with two mugs.

"I'm not one for formality, like tea sets or anything. I hope you don't mind a basic mug."

Linda took a sip and smiled. "Best coffee I've had in quite a while. Thank you." Her smile wavered, became tremulous. "Grace, I'm sorry."

"For what? Disrupting my work environment yesterday? Or for abandoning your eight-year-old daughter."

"For everything. Especially for that."

A tear slid down her mother's cheek. Grace steeled herself against the emotion. With shaking hands, her mother set her mug down. "Can I explain?"

Grace nodded, sitting back on the couch and crossing her arms in front of her, certain no explanation could erase twenty years of pain.

Her mother glanced up at the mantle again. At Grace's father, proudly standing with Grace at her white-coat ceremony, her graduation from medical school, all the pivotal points in her life. "He looks good."

Though it was a struggle, Grace managed not to scowl. Her mother didn't have the right to know how her ex-husband was doing.

"I spoke with him," Linda said.

That was a surprise. "Recently?"

"Right after Cade contacted me. I wanted to have a conversation with him before I had one with you. And I wanted his permission to talk to you. He had every right to have a say in this."

"When exactly did you speak to him?"

"Two days ago."

Last night, her father hadn't said a word other than to suggest she let her mother tell her story.

"What did he say?"

"He said the choice was yours. That he was happy now. And he wished me well."

Both Grace's eyebrows shot up. She and her father rarely talked about her mother. She'd always thought it brought up too much pain. His new love had definitely opened his eyes. She took a deep breath. Maybe it was time to open her own.

"Why did you leave? Back then. On Christmas Eve."

Linda turned toward Grace on the sofa, clutching her hands tightly in her lap. "I couldn't take it anymore."

"What?" Grace sat up as if slapped. "The responsibility?" Was that all she'd been?

"Not you," Linda said quickly. "Well, not completely. I have bipolar disorder."

Another surprise. Bipolar disorder could be dangerous. If left untreated, the highs could manifest as mania. "Dad never said anything."

"He didn't want you to know. He told me your doctor knew."

And never told her, even once she was an adult? Grace believed in honesty, brutal though it may be. She should have been told. Taking a deep breath, she reminded herself why she was here, in her living room, with the mother she said she'd never see or talk to again.

"Are you in treatment?"

"I am. Have been, for several years. Back then, though— "

Suppressed memories flew through Grace's mind. Her mother, waking her up in the middle of the night to have a tea party, laughing uncontrollably. At other times, crying. Or worse, just staring out the window at the rain. Unmoving. Why hadn't she seen it, known it?

Grace covered her mouth with a shaking hand as memories overwhelmed her.

"You couldn't have known," her mother said. "You were too young."

"Why did you leave? On Christmas Eve?"

"That was the worst possible moment to reach my limit. I know. And I know I caused you irreparable harm, but I couldn't take it anymore. The highs and lows, the fights with your father, and mostly, the confusion in your eyes. My emotions were all over the place. I couldn't eat and I was drinking heavily to self-medicate. I could no longer live with myself, with John, with you. That day, I decided to commit suicide."

Suicide. The ultimate act to escape pain. Grace's heart thumped and she almost reached out to her mother.

"In my own way, I loved you, Grace. I didn't want you to watch me die. I didn't want either of you to know about the decision I'd made. So I made up an excuse. I left your father a letter saying I wanted a better life than I could have with you. That I wanted money, which was the last thing on my mind." Tears streamed down Linda's face now. "I thought that would be better than you finding out I planned to—take my own life."

An ache, deep in Grace's soul, bubbled up until it filled her heart. She rubbed at her chest, trying to understand what her mother had gone through that day. "Were you drinking that Christmas Eve?"

Linda shook her head. "I was as clear-headed as I'd ever been."

"So suicide seemed like the only choice you had?"

A quick nod. "I don't think I can fully explain how wild bipolar episodes can get. I hated myself. Hated who I was in the throes of my illness."

"Even twenty years ago, there was medication for bipolar disorder."

"Lithium. Antipsychotics. None of them made me feel normal, or right. I'd stopped taking them, oh, around Thanksgiving that year, I believe. I hated how I felt on them. But without them, I hated myself worse."

"So you left." A trickle of compassion made its way into Grace's voice and dampened the ache in her heart.

"I left. I'm so sorry I did that to you. I handled it very badly but I didn't know what else to do. No way did I want you to see me at my worst."

"What happened after you left?"

"I went to the bridge. You know, the one you and I used to walk across every Saturday?"

Grace inhaled sharply and stared at her mother. "I know the bridge. I walked it every Saturday for months, hoping you'd come find me there."

"I wound up a long way from there. That Christmas Eve I stood on that bridge for hours, even climbed up to sit on the concrete railing." Her mother looked out the window. "In the end, I couldn't do it. I convinced myself I couldn't commit suicide on our bridge. So I caught a bus out of town."

"To where?"

"Wherever it took me. I rode busses for a week, staying in seedy motels."

"You had money?"

"I drained John's savings. It wasn't much. A couple thousand dollars. Everywhere I stopped, I set out to commit suicide, but I kept imagining the look on your face if you ever found out."

Her mother reached out to rest her hand on Grace's arm. Grace stared at it, letting the emotions swirl around her.

"You saved me every time, Grace. I need you to know that."

"But you still didn't come home."

"I didn't. By the time I gave up on the idea of suicide, I figured you were better off without me." Linda pulled her hand back. "That you'd gotten over me."

"I never did. Ever. I never got past any of it."

"I know that now. I didn't then."

"Twenty years. Where did twenty years go?"

"About ten of them went to alcohol and drugs."

Illicit drugs. A common choice for bipolar people looking to self-medicate. Grace nodded, having heard the story from patients before. Compassion for what her mother had gone through welled up in her. She could understand, but could she forgive? Highly doubtful.

"And the last ten?"

"I spent those cleaning myself up, getting steady on meds, seeing doctors and therapists. Finding myself."

"Finding yourself. But still not bothering with me."

She had to give Linda credit. The woman didn't break her gaze as she absorbed the hit. Grace looked away first.

"I know it's not enough and it's too late to make a difference, but I never once forgot about you. I followed you from afar as best I could. I was there for your graduation from the University of Washington."

Grace's head came up.

"Also for your white-coat ceremony, and your graduation from medical school."

"You were in the audience?"

Linda nodded. "I figured, with so many years gone, it would just throw you into turmoil if I re-entered your life."

Everything in Grace wanted to deny what her mother had said. She'd kept track of her? Knew she'd become a doctor and had even watched her graduate? A part of Grace wanted that time back, to know her mother had been there and was proud of her. Could they recover any part of what they'd lost? "Why now?"

"Cade. He's a very… persuasive man."

He is that. Grace got up and walked around the room, unable to equate the years of anger and hatred with the woman who sat on her couch patiently giving her time to process.

"It's a lot to take in."

"I get that." Linda rose and joined Grace at the front window. "I know I did everything wrong where you are concerned. I hurt you. Badly. I'm more sorry than I can convey. Cade said that you hate Christmas and that what happened is holding you back from having a fulfilling life, from loving."

"Cade had no right."

"He said that, too. Here's the thing. I'd like an opportunity to make it up to you, to be part of your life. But I won't force the issue. If you don't want me around, I understand. I'll leave as quietly as I entered, no harm, no foul. And right now, I'll leave you with your thoughts. You need time."

"Thank you for understanding that. I'll take you home."

"I can catch an Uber."

Grace smiled at the trace of family stubbornness peeking out from her mother's attitude. "Please don't take this the wrong way," she said, "but I get the impression you don't have a lot of money to spare. I appreciate that you're giving me time to think, but I can do that after I take you home."

Bowing her head in assent, Linda reached for her coat and purse. The drive back to the motel was quiet, but not as fraught with tension as when Grace had picked her mother up. As she got out, she turned back to Grace like she wanted to say something. Instead, she canted her head and offered a poignant smile. "Thank you." She closed the door and walked off without another word.

Drained, Grace watched her mother until the lobby door shut behind her, reminding her of another door shutting behind the same woman all those years ago. Except this time, she saw the desperate person who'd thought she had no other recourse but to protect her family by leaving. Grace pulled out slowly, heading for home. Except she didn't want to go home. Rain or not, she headed for the lookout point where Cade had taken her.

There, with the rain streaming down her windshield, Grace let her tears fall. For years she'd never cried. Now, she'd done it twice in as many days, and she couldn't stop. Everything spilled out. An eight-year-old's love that had turned to fear, then anger and hatred, eventually morphing into the resignation of an adult trying to get on with her life. She'd lived despite her mother's abandonment. Her father had done his best to give her a decent life. And Grace's life had been good. She'd made opportunities for herself, getting grants and scholarships so that her med school debt hadn't been too overwhelming. That drive to succeed had come from the insecurity of her mother's abandonment. So something good had come from it.

But twenty years. That was a lot of hurt to let go of. Grace cried for her eight-year-old self. She cried for the young lady who hadn't known her mother was in the audience at graduation, and for a mother so distraught she saw no other recourse than to leave her husband and daughter. Helpless and thinking of taking her own life.

Grace also cried for the love she'd given up in Cade.

Finally, shivering from cold, Grace's tears subsided. She started her car, turning the wipers on while waiting for the cabin to warm up. The waves were churning because of the weather. Just like her, trying to find a way to be calm. Some fool was running on the beach in the rain, in a Santa hat. Was the man crazy?

Then it hit Grace again. Today was Christmas Eve. Even as a resident, she'd always volunteered for Christmas duty. Working the holiday had been the only way to get through the pain.

Would she feel that same pain tonight? No. Grace still had a lot to sort out, but one thing she knew for certain. Tonight, the maelstrom of anger and unworthiness would not devastate her Christmas Eve. She had Cade to thank for freeing her. Cade, who thought he knew better about what she needed than she knew herself. Who may have been right, even if how he did it was wrong. Cade, who could make her laugh, who loved even her faults, who'd dragged her into Christmas whether she wanted to celebrate or not. Because of him, she had an opportunity to begin healing.

What was he doing right now? Was he celebrating with friends? Somehow, Grace didn't think so. She'd hurt him because he'd hurt her. Even after he held her through her tears, she'd lashed out. He'd handled things wrong, but his heart had been in the right place. With her. Wanting her healed and whole. God, she needed to see him. Needed to set things right. To tell him she loved him and see if maybe he could still love her.

Grace started the car and threw it into reverse, knowing what she needed to do.

Chapter Seventeen

Cade stared at the television. After a visit to the hospital to find his dad doing better and his mother ensconced at his side giving orders, Cade had settled in at home. He'd been watching *It's a Wonderful Life* for hours now. Seemed appropriate for today, except for that whole happy ending thing. Nope. Life didn't give out happy endings, and his luck had run out on designing his own.

God, he'd screwed up so bad. He knew not to push Grace too far, yet he'd taken the ultimate plunge and forced her to face the biggest wound from her past. She was a strong, independent woman and he'd forgotten that in his supreme belief that he could make everything better. Make her the whole person he knew she wanted to be. Except she didn't need his meddling. Grace had found a way to survive and be content with her life and he'd destroyed that.

And lost her in the process.

Grace would never forgive him for this. He was the worst kind of heel and he'd managed to lose a love he'd barely found. A love that had slapped him upside the face and shown him what his life had been missing when he'd thought it was complete.

He took a gulp of wine from a bottle of red he'd just opened, barely tasting it. Cade didn't usually drown his sorrows. Not like this. And damn it, wine wouldn't numb this pain. Not enough. He needed something stronger.

How was he going to live through this? He couldn't, at least not without trying to make things right. He grabbed his head, trying to think of something, anything, that would make Grace listen to him. He'd spend the rest of his life apologizing if she'd just give him the chance.

So bullheaded, thinking he could force Christmas— and the mother who'd abandoned her—on Grace. He'd listened when she said never to contact her again. He really had, except it was the hardest thing he'd ever done. Had she thought about him at all? Was she okay?

Cade needed to know like he needed air to breathe. One last time, he'd go see her. Ask to talk so he could apologize. If she didn't let him in, he'd know it was over for good.

With renewed purpose, Cade got up and reached for his coat and car keys. He raced for the door before his brain could remind him to leave the woman be. He threw the door open to a surprised Grace, her hand raised to knock.

"Grace," he said, breathing hard, barely able to fathom that she was here on his porch.

"Can we talk?"

She was here. More beautiful than ever, though he could see a puffiness around her eyes. Had she cried again? Had he caused it? He stood holding the door, staring.

"Can I come in? Cade?"

Her words filtered through the fog. "Oh, gosh, sure. Come in. God, please, come in." He wanted to sweep her into his arms as he swung the door shut, but he knew he had no right. So he did nothing more than stare at the woman he loved as every atom in his being urged him toward her.

With her free hand, Grace reached for him, then pulled back.

"I thought I'd never see you again," he said.

"Where were you going just now?"

"To find you. Even though you didn't want me to."

Grace shook her head. "It's always going to be like this with you, isn't it?"

"Like what?"

"You, steamrolling right through whatever I want because you think you know what's best."

"Probably." He smiled, the first cautious happiness he'd felt since Grace told him to leave her alone. "Sounds like you're talking about a future for us."

She pressed against his chest with her palm. "Slow down, steamroller. How about we talk some things out first, then we can talk about the future."

"Doesn't matter what we talk about. I'm in. All the way. Whatever you need me to do, I'll do. I love you, Grace. More than life, more than anything."

Her eyes widened, then she smiled. "Well, that's very nice to know, Mr. Huntington. I love you, too."

Words he'd waited his entire life to hear, though he hadn't known it. Cade reached to pull her into his embrace, frustrated when she stepped back.

"First, we talk."

Cade reined in his impatience, albeit barely. He helped her off with her coat and hung it on the coat tree near the door. "Can I get you something to drink?"

"Just some water." Grace followed him to the kitchen, sitting at the island and running her hands over the quartz countertop. "So I'm guessing you had this place remodeled when you bought it?"

"Yes. That's one of the benefits of what I make from gaming. You know me. I always want to fix things as soon as I see an issue. The money allows me to do things like this." He waved a hand around the comfortable kitchen.

"How rich are you, actually?"

He shrugged, handing her a glass of water with a lemon slice in it. "Not billionaire rich."

"So millionaire rich?"

Heat crept up his neck. "Um, several times over, yes."

Grace frowned.

"But only because I don't spend it. I don't need it, as a rule, so I invest most of it. Although, sometimes, I pay for renovations. Or nice SUVs."

"That explains how a cable guy can afford that luxury vehicle."

If this was where their conversation was starting, how much worse was it going to get? Cade fingered the dish towel laying on the counter. "Is the money a problem?"

"You know, I thought it would be. I've never wanted to be around that kind of money. In fact, I kind of despise rich people. Or did."

His hand froze on the towel. "Did?"

"Recent… events have skewed my thinking some."

"So now you like rich people?" Cade rounded the island to stand in front of her.

"Down, boy."

He did just that, sitting next to her, facing her, reaching for her hand.

"I talked to my mother this morning."

"You did?"

"Yes. And while I still believe you were wrong to interfere, especially after I told you not to, some things she said revealed that my assumptions were invalid."

"How so?"

"My mother didn't run because of money, although that's what the note she left my dad said. At the time, she thought that would be easier on us than her real plans."

"Which were?" Cade had vetted Grace's mom to be sure she truly wanted to reconcile, but hadn't asked for any explanations.

"She'd planned to commit suicide."

Whoa. That was unexpected. Cade stroked Grace's hands. "That must have been hard to hear."

Grace stared at their intertwined hands, nodding. "She's bipolar. Do you know what that means?"

"Emotional highs and lows, right?"

"Yes. Exceptional highs and deep depression on the other end. Cade?"

"What? What is it? He thought he saw fear in her eyes.

"Bipolar disease can be hereditary."

Cade stopped stroking her hand and took a few moments to digest the information. "You mean, when we have kids, we'll have to keep an eye out for those highs and lows?"

"Well, that's part of it."

"I'm up to the task."

"I believe it." Grace looked away. "I could be affected, Cade. I could be bipolar."

He turned her face back to him, making sure she saw the truth in his eyes. "If that happens, we'll deal with it together."

"My mother has been to hell and back. Dad, too. I'm not sure I should risk putting you through that."

"Putting us through that." He grinned. "Kind of sounds like you're making decisions for me that I want to make myself."

The hint of a smile tugged at Grace's lips. "Touché."

"How did you leave things with your mother?"

"I asked for some time. I want to put this all behind us but I'm not there yet."

"Your kind of hurt doesn't go away overnight."

"Agreed. It's going to take some time." Grace tightened her hold on Cade's hands. "I'm ready to work on it now. Thanks to you."

Cade saw the honesty in her eyes. Saw the truth there. "I know you are."

He thought she might give him a full smile this time, but her eyes turned wary. "You're not off the hook yet, mister. Us, giving this another try, doesn't mean you can *ever* do something like this to me again. I lost power over my life all those years ago. It hurt, losing it again through your actions. I need you to understand that."

A tear fell. A tear of sadness he'd created through his actions. He was the worst kind of heel. "How about we make a pact?"

"What kind of pact?"

"I won't go off half-cocked without talking to you."

"And I will listen to what you have to say without an immediate rejection."

"Look at us," he said, grinning. "We're working things out."

"Somehow, I don't think our life will be boring, Cade Huntington."

He released her hands to hold his up in the air. "I'm a reformed man."

"Somehow, I doubt that."

Grace's laughter rolled over, under, and through Cade, straight to his soul, settling everything in his world.

~~~

"So we're good, right?" Cade asked. "We're going to see where this thing goes?"

Well. It might be a touch late, but his concern for her, making sure she was on the same page before proceeding, lightened her heart. "Oh, yes," she said, sliding closer to him. "We're good. We're very, very good."

That slow, sexy smile she loved spread across his

face. With a tenderness that almost brought Grace to tears, Cade ran a hand along her hair, cupped her cheek, and leaned in to touch his lips to hers.

Gentle gave way to a craving that had only gotten stronger. She deepened the kiss, reveling in the feel of his lips on hers. Cade tangled his hands in her hair, bringing her in tighter. She pressed against him, needing more, wanting so much all at once.

Together, they danced, lips, tongues, hands. She couldn't get enough of him. When Cade broke the kiss, Grace moaned, breathing hard. Same as Cade.

"How about— " His voice cracked. "How about we take this to the bedroom?"

"Finally!" Grace said, jumping up.

Cade laughed and stood, grabbing her hand and leading her upstairs to his bedroom. Beside the bed, he kissed her again, turning her bones to jelly. She could hardly stand. He kissed her cheek, moved to her neck, and nibbled on her ear, sending thrills straight through to her core. Stilling her when she tried to sit down, Cade whispered in her ear.

"Let me get you out of these clothes."

Everything inside her perked up at the idea. He unbuttoned her blouse with agonizing leisure, kissing each bit of skin he bared. Grace tugged at his t-shirt, trying to speed things up.

"Sit," he said, stepping back to pull his shirt over his head.

Grace touched the light patch of hair over his chest to caress his nipples and run her hands along taut muscles.

"Still my turn," Cade said, slipping her blouse off and tossing it behind him. For once, Grace didn't care that it might get wrinkled. Nothing mattered but Cade. Here. Now. In this moment.

"A front clasp. I like those." With one deft flick, her

bra opened and joined the clothing pile on the floor. He stood there for so long staring at her that Grace licked her lips nervously. Did he like what he saw? The man was so fit, so perfectly formed, and every one of her flaws flashed through her mind.

"Wow," he said.

"Good wow?"

"Of course, good wow." Cade knelt in front of her. "Spectacular wow. How can you think otherwise?"

"My breasts are too small."

Eye-level with her chest, he cupped them both, shaking his head. "They are the perfect size. Look how they fit in my hand."

Grace had had sex before, of course, but always in darkened rooms. Never with the overhead light on. And she'd never watched, or even looked. Glancing down, she was mesmerized as Cade's hands caressed her, sending tingles through her body and heating the very center of her being.

When he took a nipple in his mouth, she moaned in pure bliss.

He pulled back. "Perfect," he whispered, then took the other nipple in his mouth, his hand caressing the one left behind. Bracing her arms on the bed behind her, Grace arched into him, wanting more. Needing more.

"Cade— "

"We've waited a long time for this, sweetheart. I want to know every part of you, body and soul, in intimate detail." He stood, guided her upright, then pulled her yoga pants off almost as slowly as he had her shirt. When he kissed the white patch of her panties, Grace jumped at the shock that raced through her.

"Now, your pants," she said.

"Oh, yeah." Cade unbuttoned his jeans and yanked them and his boxers off in one swoop. Grace licked her lips again. The man was magnificent. And huge. And proudly at attention. She wanted his cock, him, inside her, filling her.

In no time at all, they were on the bed and Cade began his exploration anew, running his hands down her arms and back up the inside, along the side of her torso. She shivered.

"Ticklish?"

"Not until now."

He grinned at her, his eyes bright with desire. Running his fingers lightly across her nipple, she gasped and arched into him. Feather touches ran along her stomach and lower. Grace writhed with need.

"Cade," she begged. "Please."

His hand continued its gentle movements, with no regard for her aching need to bring him inside her. "So beautiful," he murmured.

Grace reached between them and grasped him. He gasped and pulled back. "In a hurry?"

"Yes. We've got our entire lives to explore. I need you. Now." She gripped his arms, trying to get her point across.

"As my lady wishes," he said, reaching behind him for a condom.

She took it out of his hand, ripped it open, and stared at him for a long moment.

~~~

Cade could see the challenge in Grace's eyes. His cock twitched as she ever so slowly rolled the condom down his length. Then she surprised him, standing on the bed, her panties right in front of him. He leaned in, grabbed a hold of them with his teeth, and pulled. With her help, they were quickly disposed of. Reaching for her hips, he pulled her close before she could get away, sinking his tongue into her.

"Oh my God," she cried, spreading her legs.

He circled her clit, his tongue roaming across her

most sensitive parts until her legs shook.

"Lay down," he said.

She did, and he moved between her legs, centering himself, his arms holding him over her. Cade leaned in, kissing Grace deeply as he plunged inside, the heady feeling of her arching into him making him twitch with need. She felt so good, begging him to move with her body.

Ask and you shall receive. He pulled out, then plunged back in, filling her, loving the tight feel, letting the friction build between them.

Faster, faster, he pounded. Grace met each thrust. He held himself over her, saw the love mingled with lust in her eyes, open for him to see with no reserve. A look meant only for him. She was his as much as he was hers.

With one hand, he reached in to press a thumb to her clit. Grace screamed her climax, with Cade following close behind. "Grace," he yelled as he spilled into the condom, his heart pounding, his legs and arms wobbly with exhaustion.

Bringing her in close to him, he lay on his side, unwilling to pull out of her soft, all-encompassing sheath.

"Wow," she said, squirming against him.

"Yeah. Fucking wow. Stars are still circling over my head." She'd given everything to him, torn down every wall, every defense, and let him see her soul. His reaction to her trust had been the most emotional ride of his life.

"Are you crying?"

Cade sniffed. "Not that anyone but you will ever know. I love you, and it's stronger than anything I've ever felt before. It took this, making love, to a whole new level. I'm humbled by it."

Grace reached up to caress his cheek. "I feel the same way. I've waited so long for you to come into my life. The love I feel for you, it tears everything down and rebuilds the world into a bigger, brighter place. Thank you. For loving me. For waiting until I could love you back."

"I want you with me forever, Grace Benson. Say you'll stay."

She tucked her head into his neck. Cade held his breath waiting for her reply. When it came, the last puzzle piece of his life slipped into place.

"There's nowhere else I'd rather be."

Lifting her chin, he kissed her with gentle abandon, filling it with all his love. And feeling that love returned.

When he broke the kiss, he hugged her tight, her arms just as tight around him.

"Want to go take a shower?" he asked.

"Sounds good to me, as long as we're together."

~~~

While Cade disposed of the condom and warmed the water, Grace looked in the mirror, touching well-loved lips, the rosy rash of Cade's stubble across her chest, nipples ripe and still wanting his touch. His arms slipped around her and he cupped her breasts, toying with the tips until she arched into his hands.

"I get lost in you," she said, turning in his embrace to kiss him and then stepping back into his free-standing shower. Cade guided her into the stream and cupped her ass, kissing her as the warm water flowed over both of them. He nudged her until the shower wall stopped her, then hit a button, turning the water to a hot mist. He dropped to his knees.

His fingers parted her. Grace dug her hands in his hair as he brought her to the edge again. He drove a finger inside and she moaned in ecstasy. Then two fingers, curving them, hitting her most vulnerable spot while he sucked.

Grace exploded into a million tiny pieces of light, ethereal, floating, riding on air and mist. Cade stood, holding her tenderly while she came back down to earth.

"I love watching you come apart for me."

"Only for you," she said, kissing him. "Only for you." With his need pulsing against her stomach, Grace grinned and nudged him back. "Got another one of those condoms?" She turned and, putting her hands on the shelf, bent over, opening herself to him.

He stepped out of the shower for a moment. When he returned, the rip of a packet told her he would answer her need. Within moments, he'd eased back inside her, filling her, touching her core, and causing desire to thread its way through her yet again.

Leaning over her, he cupped her breast with one hand, tucking his other finger along her clit, sliding with the same rhythm as his cock. His breath quickened, hers right along with his. Soon, with both hands on her hips, he pounded into her. In, out. Filling her, hitting every erotic nerve, hitting her soul as she flew again.

With a groan, he let go, pulsing inside her, his hands running up and down her back then around her waist, supporting her body, fall-down drunk on pleasure.

"Merry Christmas, my love," Cade said.

She'd completely forgotten. Christmas Day had arrived, and what a Christmas it was. He turned the spray back on and they washed, dried, and were soon snuggled in Cade's bed. No emergency room shift had ever worn Grace out like this. Yet it was a different kind of tired. A sated and happy kind. Grace knew she would no longer spend Christmas bemoaning her childhood, hiding away from the season, not letting herself get involved. In the holidays, or her job.

"Do you have enough food to throw together a dinner? Let's invite your mom over for Christmas. We can visit your dad in the hospital then bring her home with us," she said, snuggling against him. "I'm so glad the damage to his heart wasn't as extensive as they first thought."

"Me, too. And I think having Mom here is a good idea. A distraction for her."

"Yes. I think your parents deserve to know we're back to being a couple." The kernel of an idea had formed in Grace's mind, but she wanted to think it through before she broached the subject. "And let's invite Lin—my mom, too."

"Wow," Cade said, tightening his hold on Grace.

"It's time to put the past behind me."

"Now that's the best Christmas present I've ever gotten," Cade said.

Chapter Eighteen

Things couldn't have turned out better if Cade had planned them. Oh, wait, he had planned them. He'd envisioned this when he'd gone searching for Grace's mother. Granted, there had been a few bumps along that road. He'd been a bit too headstrong for his own good, but it had all turned out, and so well.

They'd stopped at Grace's place so she could change. Cade fed Luna and the cat rubbed up against him like she'd known him for years. Apparently, that hatchet had been buried. Even better, Dad had looked much improved when they'd visited him. He'd be coming home in a couple days, then starting cardiac rehab. His days at the clinic were done but he'd taken the news well. Eventually, Cade's mother would retire, too. They both wanted to take life easier. That was Cade's next problem to solve. Finding doctors to staff the clinic. There would be no more stress-related health issues on his watch.

After Grace had called her mother to invite her to dinner, she'd picked her up, along with the town's wanderer and matchmaker, Gladys, while he'd prepared the food. Now, Linda stood chatting with his mother while Grace and Gladys set the table.

Grace came up behind him as he stirred the au jus

for the prime rib. Hugging him, she heaved a happy sigh. "This is so nice."

"I'd rather we were alone."

She nuzzled his back. "We hopefully have lots of time for that."

"Not enough." He turned and pulled her into his arms for a long kiss, then handed her the spatula. "Stir, while I carve the main course and get the food on the table."

They worked side by side at the island in companionable silence and he watched their mothers having an animated conversation about clinic work. Turned out, Grace's mother was a receptionist in a mental health clinic in Portland.

"You two look good working there together," Gladys said, plopping down on a stool on the far side of the island. "I'm glad you finally figured out you were meant to be together."

"Seems like we had a lot of people pulling for us. Not the least of which was you."

Gladys patted her white hair, preening. "I've got great instincts." She picked up her glass of whiskey and walked straight and tall across the room to the others. "Yesiree, great instincts."

"I've been thinking about something," Grace said after Gladys had wandered off.

"What's that?" Still distracted by how well the two mothers and Gladys were getting along, Cade missed Grace's next words. "What?"

"I said, I think I'd like to switch to clinical medicine."

He paused, the knife in mid-cut, and looked at her for a long beat. "Are you seriously going to go to work for my parents?"

Grace shrugged. "Emergency room work isn't the be-all and end-all I thought it would be. Working for your parents would get me out of the ER and solve their staffing problem. Kind of feels like a win-win to me. Besides, I think I could get used to holidays off." She looked around the room, content with Christmas for the first time, and happy to be surrounded by people.

"You don't know what you're getting into. My parents will run roughshod over you and we'll never have a life of our own."

"Oh, I think I can hold my own with your parents."

"Of course, you can, dear," his mother said, standing on the other side of the island, smiling like the Cheshire Cat.

"You heard?" Cade said, squinting.

"How could I not?" She came around the island and hugged Grace. "Welcome to the family, Dr. Benson. At least, the clinic family." She broke the hug and gave Cade a pointed look.

Grace's laughter fed his soul.

"Come on. Time to eat," he said.

Before long, they were passing food around, filling their plates. When Grace lifted the basket of rolls, she gasped to find a small box sitting behind it.

Gladys squealed with pleasure.

"Merry Christmas, Grace," Cade said.

"This can't be what it looks like. We barely know each other."

Cade reached for her hand. "It's not. I know better—now—than to throw something like that at you suddenly and in a crowd."

She opened the festive box, pulled out the smaller ring box, and opened it to find a rich garnet ring rimmed with diamonds and set in warm gold. "It's beautiful, Cade."

"It's a promise from me to you. A pledge. I will always try to find a compromise. I will never surprise you unless I'm absolutely certain you'll like it—like right now—and I will love you for all of our time together."

"And tell me you love me every day?" She leaned in and touched his cheek.

"Always."

"Thank you, Cade." She slipped the ring on her left ring finger. "I'll treasure this." She chewed her lip. "I didn't get anything for you."

"You are all the gift I need."

Everything around them faded as he kissed her. When they turned around, three women sat there grinning like fools. Since Cade figured he had the same stupid grin on his face, he just grabbed his fork.

"Dig in, everyone."

Epilogue

Cade slipped into the emergency room among the chaos of New Year's Eve revelers. He didn't get too far. Nurse Stan whipped around a stretcher bearing a drunk person in a mardi-gras mask holding his strangely canted shoulder.

Stan put a hand out to stop Cade. "Last time you were here, you made her cry. She's only got a few more days. No way am I letting you ruin them."

"I'm not going to ruin them, I swear." Cade offered his best trust-me grin.

"Yeah, well, you're ruining them for me. She's one of the best ER docs I've ever worked with."

"I thought she'd been nicknamed the Ice Queen?" Nothing could be further from the truth. Grace was warm, loving, and passionate, especially in the bedroom. If they only knew what she was capable of. His smile widened.

"I hate that nickname," Stan said with a grimace. "Those people never took the time to get to know Dr. Benson, or how to work with her. And now, you're taking her away from us."

Cade held up the two big bags he carried. "I've brought a peace offering."

Judging by the look on Stan's face, nothing would change his opinion of Cade. He peeked in one of the bags then back up at Cade, reluctantly giving the man credit. "Leave it to you to find the one thing that we can't refuse. Go ahead. Set them in the break room." Stan stepped to the side just as paramedics burst through the doors with another stretcher, this one marked with a significant amount of blood.

Walking over to lean against the wall, Cade watched the chaotic action around him. Grace walked out of one room to triage the newest patient right there in the hallway, barking orders like the professional she was. Everyone scattered to follow those orders as Grace joined him, perfectly calm as if there weren't a plethora of patients all needing attention.

"Hi," she whispered, leaning in for a kiss.

Unable to think about anything but kissing her more—and everywhere—Cade held up the bags. "I brought pies for everyone."

"Oooh, nice. Best pies around, too."

"Thought it might melt the attitudes. Stan thinks I'm stealing you away."

Grace laughed. "You are. Well, your folks are."

He moved the bags to one hand and reached up to tuck in a stray strand of hair that had come loose from her bun. "Only a few more days and you'll be in clinical work."

Her eyes shone. "I'm looking forward to it."

"And my parents finally get a doctor in the family."

She glanced down at the garnet on her ring finger. "Not quite family."

"Oh, that promise is real. We're getting married and you won't be able to talk me out of it."

"Not that I'd ever want to," she said. "But no surprise weddings. This time, we plan together."

"You've got it."

"Dr. Benson?" Stan called from the med station.

"Duty calls," Grace said, giving him a quick kiss before turning to see what new emergency had arisen.

Cade watched her walk away, unsure how he'd gotten lucky enough to snag the best woman in the whole wide world. Smart, beautiful, and strong. Everything he loved, and he planned to show her how much he loved her every day for the rest of their lives.

Yep. He was a lucky man. As he headed for the breakroom to set out the pies and the Happy New Year sign he'd drawn up, Cade whistled a soft, happy tune. Life was good, and it would only get better from here.

They'd share everything. Together. Forever.

~~~

Thank you for reading **Reluctant Christmas**, the fifth story in the *Willow Bay* series. While this series can be read in any order, the next one in the series is **Operation Ethan** (Rule following Firefighter Ethan Walker meets his match in happy-go-lucky Joey Sanderson.) If you enjoyed this book, please consider leaving a review wherever you prefer, and know that it would be greatly appreciated.

For new release information and news about Laurie Ryan, please join her newsletter at: www.laurieryanauthor.com.

Note/Acknowledgements

I can't imagine not loving Christmas, except for religious reasons and I respect those differences greatly. Growing up, my mother made sure, even with her limited means, that Christmas was fun for all five of us kids.

Christmas eve was bath night, then she would pin curl my hair, as well as my two sisters'. The next morning, brightly eyeing all the presents under the tree, we could only open the one in our stocking. Then the pin curls came out, hair was brushed, my brothers were corralled into some semblance of order, and off to church we went.

After church, you'd think it was time to open gifts. Nope. We cooked a full-on ham and egg breakfast, ate, AND did the dishes before FINALLY sitting down to open gifts.

It seemed like torture back then, but now it is a treasured memory. I hope you all have a season or holiday that carries that kind of special love.

Libby Doyle, as always, you polished me to a fine art. Thank you! And **Cari Friesen**, your cover for these books are spectacular! You read my mind.

As always, I couldn't do this without my critique team. **Lavada Dee, Faye Avalon, Sadira Stone, Marie Tuhart**, you always help me see things clearly.

Booklist

Contemporary romance stories by Laurie Ryan

Willow Bay Series
Last Resort
Finding Home
Chances Are
Tender Tide
Reluctant Christmas
Operation Ethan

Tropical Persuasions Series
Stolen Treasures
Pirate's Promise
Dare to Love

Standalone
Rudy's Heart
Lost and Found
Northern Lights
Healing Love
(also part of the Holiday Magic anthology)

Women's Fiction by Laurie Ryan
Show Me

Fantasy by Laurie Ryan
Survival
Enlightenment
Birthright
Awakening
Wolf's Call

Author Bio

Laurie Ryan writes fantasy and contemporary romance. Growing up a devoted reader, Laurie Ryan immersed herself in the diverse works of authors like Tolkien and Woodiwiss. She is passionate about every aspect of a book: beginning, middle, and end. She can't arrive to a movie five minutes late, has never been able to read the end of a book before the beginning, and is a strong believer in reading the book before seeing the movie.

Laurie lives in the beautiful Pacific Northwest, in the shadow of Mt. Rainier and a short drive to beach-walking next to the Pacific Ocean, with her handsome, he-can-fix-anything husband.

You can find more about Laurie Ryan at:

www.laurieryanauthor.com

A Sneak Peek at the Sixth Book in the Willow Bay Series

Operation Ethan
by Laurie Ryan

Chapter One

"You've got to be kidding me." Joey stared at Pacific Lodge's head of maintenance, looking around the comfortable, upscale lobby to make sure no one heard.

"Not kidding," John said. "Room 302 got completely flooded and won't be usable for at least two to three weeks. We can fix the one below that in a few days, though. But 402, where the leak came from, also needs quite a bit of work." John ran a hand through his short salt-and-pepper hair making it stand up even more than usual.

"The Beer and Chowder Festival is in ten days and we're booked solid. We cannot lose a room."

"Then maybe you should convince your guests to stand inside the tub to shower, not outside."

Joey tucked blonde hair behind an ear, rolling her eyes at having been called downstairs at midnight last night when guests complained of water dripping from the ceiling over their bed. Turns out, the couple in the room above came from a country where bathing was different. They'd filled the tub then stood on the bathroom floor pouring water over themselves. That water had buckled the ceiling in the room below. Now ceiling, floors, walls, furniture—it all needed fixed.

"Thank God the couple below got out of bed before the sheetrock fell."

"There is that." She sent a prayer skyward for the blessing.

Joey looked around the lobby of the five-story lodge. Pride filled her at the serenity and beauty, decorated in mellow, pleasing tans accented with ocean colors. Deep blue, sea green, and white. Guests complimented her on the ambiance of the place and pride filled her every time she walked in here.

Back to the problem at hand. Having to cancel one reservation wouldn't go over well with the owners. The loss of two would make the bottom-line focused Christian Reynolds the First, apoplectic. Taking a moment to picture his red, puffy face, his gray hair just about turning white as he sputtered his indignation, brought the smile back to Joey's face. It faded quickly when she glanced at the revolving door entrance.

"Speak of the devil." Her worst nightmare had just walked in and stood looking around with his permanent frown firmly in place.

Joey turned back to John. "Get the top room working within two days. I don't care what you have to do, what laws you break, or what it costs. Get. It. Done. Now. Go."

Joey flipped around, pasting the smile on her face that had gotten her this job, and watched as Mr. Reynolds strode her way. Out of the corner of her eye, she saw Gladys, Willow Bay's sweet, resident, elder street person, set her cart beside the door. *Not now, Gladys. Please, not now.* With her pleas unheard, Gladys, who seemed to wear every bit of clothing she owned, stepped lively through the revolving door and straight to a nearby settee where she liked to "rest her bones" on her daily journey. Joey never minded. Gladys had a wealth of information about the happenings around Willow Bay and Joey enjoyed talking to her. Or would at any other time.

Facing the challenge head on, Joey met her boss at the large round table that was the centerpiece of the lobby, a large vase of cut flowers reminding folks that spring would return.

"Mr. Reynolds, it's lovely to see you again this week, though I can't imagine that rain made for a very nice drive."

"It didn't. And I'm none too pleased to be here instead of at my club, but this was an errand I wanted to do in person." He glanced beyond her to what she knew was John's retreating backside. "Why were you talking to maintenance?"

Joey crossed her fingers behind her back. "I check in with each department every day to stay on top of things."

"Hmph. Good idea." Though the rare compliment was grumbled out like it wasn't easy for him to say. "Flowers?" he said, looking at the vase.

"From a local florist. They make folks smile and remember better weather."

"Hmph. And these brochures?" He picked up a stack and thumbed through them.

"Information about points of interest, tours, gift shops, etc. around town."

He plucked out a Square Peg Pizza menu—her favorite restaurant—and held it up. "Don't we have a restaurant?"

"Well, yes, but—"

"Then we don't need to advertise other restaurants,

do we?"

Heat flooded Joey's cheeks and she bit the inside of her mouth to keep from saying what was on her mind. "This is a small community." She'd learned that quickly wandering around her first week here. "We advertise for each other. Square Peg, for instance, has Pacific Lodge brochures out in their restaurant."

"But they're not a hotel, they're an eatery." He threw the brochures in the garbage can below the table. "I bought this place as an investment and I expect it to perform, not send guests to other venues."

"Customer satisfaction is at the highest it has ever been, Mr. Reynolds. Things like these brochures help with that rating. I'm sure you understand how important reviews are to this business and ours have been great the last couple months. Even with winter upon us, we're three-quarters full or above at all times."

"Yes, well, let's try to bump that up. And while we're talking about this, I'll need one of the penthouse suites and two other rooms for the upcoming festival."

"The—" Joey froze. Her brain melted into a pile of seagull poop at her feet and she couldn't think of a damn thing to say.

Mr. Reynolds watched her closely. Was he waiting for her to fail? Trying to force that issue?

"Pacific Lodge is completely booked for the festival, including both penthouses. People made reservations months in advance."

As his scowl darkened, Joey raced to find a solution. "With that large a party, how about I search for a house rental?" That wouldn't be easy, either. "I'm sure it would be more relaxing to be all together."

"Absolutely not. I will stay in my hotel and nowhere else."

Joey switched gears. "You'll be giving up revenue by kicking people out of their rooms. And the negative publicity could have far-reaching effects."

"That's your problem, not mine. One penthouse suite and two rooms for Friday through Monday. Or both penthouses. Either will work. I'll be back that Friday with my family." He grabbed up the rest of the brochures and handed them to Joey, turning to leave.

Joey inwardly groaned when he zeroed in on Gladys and turned back to Joey.

"Street people in our lobby? Absolutely not. Get rid of that...woman. And no brochures unless they are touting what we have to offer." He left without another glance at anything but the door.

Joey stood there, clutching the brochures until they bent. Fuming. She wanted to stomp her feet like Baby on that bridge who couldn't get the dance moves right. She allowed herself one tiny stomp. It wasn't enough, but it would have to do. She'd come here two months ago with a shiny new hotel management degree and a desperate need for a job. After three years of online classes, moving around, and looking over her shoulder, the peace of Willow Bay had settled her. In fact, already tired of living in the provided hotel room, Joey had been thinking about searching for a condo or small house to buy. Making a go of this job meant Willow Bay could be home and she wanted that very much.

She'd been welcomed here. Sam at the grocery store now stocked her favorite yogurt, having noticed her dawdling around the dairy aisle and asking. The mayor had immediately enlisted her help with the Beer and Chowder Festival and she'd met a lot of the community through related meetings.

Rescuing the brochures from the garbage, she smoothed them all out and laid them back on the table, smiling with satisfaction.

Mr. Reynolds didn't understand what made Willow Bay so special. He didn't get the small-town community feel that people came here to experience. And he sure as heck didn't understand reservations and what breaking them meant.

With one more defiant little stomp, Joey walked over to see Gladys. No way would she kick this nice, down-on-her-luck woman out. Joey would quit first. Stopping short, Joey's heartrate spiked. She couldn't quit. She needed this job.

Rock and a hard place. That phrase had a whole new meaning these days.

~~~

Gladys Hawthorne sat and watched the goings on, her ears perked in the direction of her nice friend. Joey stiffened as the older gentleman, presumably the lodge owner, tossed papers in the trash.

"Street people in our lobby? Absolutely not. Get rid of that…woman."

Pompous ass. Gladys glared at the man as he strode out. This was exactly why she left New York. She'd become fed up with that kind of holier than thou attitude from her husband's cronies. Men and women who'd called her their friend right up until she'd taken things in a direction that wasn't theirs. More pompous asses. This one went through the revolving door so fast, it almost hit him in said ass. Gladys smiled. Too bad that didn't actually happen.

Gladys's smile widened when the cute manager plucked the papers out of the garbage and smoothed them out on the table. Joey had guts and Gladys liked that in a woman.

"How are you doing today?" Joey asked as Gladys patted the seat beside her and Joey sat down.

"Much better now that I've seen your smile. You light up a room, young lady."

Joey grinned. "Why thank you. You always know how to brighten my day with the right words."

"I guess that makes us both happy people, then."

Joey laughed, a lilting sound that settled like a warm blanket around Gladys's heart.

"Your husband is lucky to have you," Gladys said. No ring didn't necessarily mean unmarried and Gladys decided that was important to clarify.

"No husband. Not yet anyhow."

"Not even a boyfriend?" Gladys's eyes gleamed.

A brief shadow touched Joey's face. So brief, Gladys almost missed it. Gladys knew about regrets and hoped this young woman didn't have the ones she herself carried.

"No. I'm pretty married to this lodge at the moment."

"But you still find time to get out and enjoy life." Joey wouldn't have her air of perennial joy if there wasn't balance in her life.

"Oh, yes. I think it's important to include both work and fun in my life."

Gladys patted her arm. "Good attitude. That'll keep you young."

"Like it has you," Joey said as she covered Gladys's hand with hers and looked her over. "You doing okay? Do you need anything? A place to rest? Some lunch?"

"What? You're not kicking me out like that stuffy boss of yours said to?"

"Never. You are welcome here anytime. You are part of what makes Willow Bay so special and I look forward to our visits."

She meant it, too. Gladys had been watching Joey for a while. The girl generally took people at face value and tried to be uplifting. She also wore her emotions on her face, and there was a wariness at the edges of the girl, like something haunted her. She needed someone to help her break through that final doorway and come fully into herself.

"I don't need anything to eat, but thank you for offering." Gladys stood. "I've had my rest and now I can get on with my day."

"You can stay longer, you know."

"I know, and I appreciate it. This was the perfect amount of time to regenerate my energy." Gladys patted Joey's cheek. "You keep on being you, being happy. The rest will sort itself out in time."

A confused look furrowed Joey's brow for a moment. She said her goodbyes and walked back behind the front desk to talk to the red-headed woman working there. All that sunshine and fun-loving was wasted here, Gladys thought. The girl needed a project that fed her soul.

Gladys knew exactly what, or who, fit that bill. With a secret smile whose meaning only she knew, she stopped at the red "Pull Down" sign on the fire alarm box. Her grin widened as she yanked the lever down and slipped out of the building, walking off to the blaring of fire alarm signals.

And feeling very, very pleased with herself.

~ ~ ~

For more information about Operation Ethan, visit Laurie Ryan's website at **www.laurieryanauthor.com**.